"I could do that!"

"Gran, look! Look at these girls. Quick! Quick!"

Gran bustled into the living room, surprised at the look of intensity on Anda's face. Together they watched a little Russian girl on the beam.

"Oh yes," said Gran. "I love to watch the gymnastics!"

"Gymnastics?" repeated Anda, tasting the word for the first time. At school they did PE or Music and Movement, both of which she enjoyed, but never anything quite like that! In herself Anda knew she could do some of the things the Olympic girls were doing!

"I could do that!" she said excitedly.

Other **Apple** paperbacks
you will enjoy:

—The—
Little
Gymnast

Sheila Haigh

AN
APPLE
PAPERBACK

SCHOLASTIC INC.
New York Toronto London Auckland Sydney

Library of Congress Cataloging-in-Publication Data

Haigh, Sheila.
The little gymnast.

Summary: With a lot of work and determination, Anda becomes the
best gymnast in her class but family money is tight and she must win
the regional championship and the accompanying scholarship or give
up gymnastics completely.
        [1. Gymnastics–Fiction. 2. England–Fiction] I. Title.
PZ7.H1263Li 1987   [Fic]   86-20206
                  ISBN 0-590-40494-6

12 11 10 9 8 7 6 5 4 3 2 1   7 8 9/8 0 1 2/9

Printed in the U.S.A.   11

First Scholastic Printing, January 1987

A Note to Readers

THE LITTLE GYMNAST was written about an English girl, and many of the gymnastics terms used in the book are British instead of American or Canadian. Here is a list of all the gymnastics terms in the book, and explanations of what each move or term means. American/Canadian "translations" of British terms are given in parentheses.

Backward roll—A continuous movement backward after the body is made into a ball by squatting and tucking.

Back straddle roll—A variation of the backward roll where the legs are spread apart and the body rolls through the legs.

Balance beam—A long piece of wood approximately 16 feet in length and 4 to 6 inches square.

Barani *(Baroni)*–An aerial round-off or front somersault with a half twist.

Buck, Vaulting Buck *(Horse, Vaulting Horse)*—A long, rectangular block of wood, covered in leather, in the shape of a horse.

Cartwheel—A stretching, rolling motion from hand to hand to foot to foot.

Crash mat *(Mat)*—Padded mat on which gymnasts land after vaulting or dismounting.

Dive roll—Forward roll started from a standing or running-jump position.

Flic-flac *(Flip-flop)*—Series of running somies (flips), performed in a floor routine.

Forward roll—A roll from a squat position over the head onto the back and seat, ending on the feet.

Handspring—An aerial flip where the hands are used to propel the body over.

Pike position—Legs straight and parallel.

Reuther board *(Beat board, spring board)*—A piece of equipment used by gymnasts to spring onto the beam, horse, or parallel bars.

Round-off—A cartwheel with a half turn and a double leg snap down.

Somie, somersault *(Flip)*—An aerial forward roll.

Straddle position—Legs spread apart.

Tinsica—A move that combines features of the cartwheel and the front walkover, starting sideways like a cartwheel, and ending front, like a front walkover.

Yamashita—A vault where a straight body is maintained into the vault, followed by a handstand from the horse to a pike position and landing.

Walkover—A move that can be performed forward or backward, which starts in a handstand, propels forward with the legs split, and ends in an upright position.

Contents

*To the little gymnasts
of Meare School, Somerset*

1

Child on the Roof

Anda Barnes rubbed her hands on the back of her jeans. There was only one way up to the church roof. Up the drainpipe. She shook it, feeling its age and its rust. A man's weight might have torn it from the wall, but it was strong enough for a girl as small as Anda.

Leaning back and pressing her sneakers into the wall, she went up like a spiderman. She put her arms round a stone gargoyle that looked down at her. With a heave and wriggle she was on the roof, her heart beating against the mossed tiles.

Above her the branch of a tall beech tree swept and dipped in the wind. Earlier that day a tiny black and white kitten had climbed the tree and made its way along the branch, looking for a way down. The thin twigs had bent, tipping the kitten on to the roof, leaving it stranded.

Now it clung, black-eyed and loud-voiced, on the apex of the roof. Its meows had filled the village and someone had called the fire department.

But it seemed to Anda that the fire department was not going to turn out for one tiny ball of meowing fluff on the church roof. So she decided to rescue it herself.

There was the roof going steeply up toward the sky. Anda had lost sight of the kitten, which was on the other side of the bell tower. She lay on her stomach and crawled up the roof bit by bit.

The watching crowd saw a head appear over the crest of the roof. They cheered. Someone must have got a ladder! Then they fell silent. The blonde head with its twirl of hair and birdlike face belonged to a child in blue jeans and a blue track suit top.

"My God, there's a child up there!"

"Go back, you silly little girl!" bellowed a big round man, waving fat hands at Anda. "No one in their right mind would get up there!"

"Don't tell her to go back! She'll fall. Keep still!" shrieked an old lady.

"Who is it? Whose little girl is that?"

"It's the child from that tumble-down cottage out at Hooty Combe," said the old lady. "I'll bet her parents don't know where she is!"

"They keep goats," said a little boy. "And chickens. I seen 'em."

2

Anda kept crawling, ignoring their shouts. A rush of rain pelted the leafy churchyard. The wet roof shone bright and slippery. Carefully Anda stood up. The next bit was easy. A narrow ledge ran along the top, straight to the bell tower. She stepped down and balance-walked quickly along it.

"Anda, come down!"

"Anda, don't go any further."

Shouts like that echoed all through her life! For Anda had always loved to climb things. Trees, rocks, buildings. She was forever getting into trouble for it.

The bell tower was more difficult. It involved going down the roof, and along, then up again. She slid down, making the seat of her jeans wet, then flattened herself against the lichened stones of the tower and began to creep sideways. Her feet were at the most impossible angle, and there was nothing to hold on to. What a long way to the ground! Just a slide, a roll and down, down, down on to the hard flag stones.

The siren of the fire engine was blasting down the steep twisting hill into Elmsford. Anda hesitated, her legs aching with the effort of staying upright. Would she make it?

There was the kitten! A scrap of fluff at the other end of the roof.

"I'll get you. Don't worry, little cat!" whispered Anda. "Little baby cat!"

Thankfully she made it to the corner of the tower and was soon crawling up again. Getting back with the kitten would be worse, unless there was another way down.

The kitten saw Anda, and opened its little pink mouth in a silent meow! It had cried itself hoarse.

On wobbly legs it walked along the roof toward her. Incredibly, the point of its tail was up and the little face bright.

"That's right! Come on. Come to me, baby cat!" she crooned. And the kitten came straight to her. Sitting astride the roof, Anda picked it up. It weighed nothing! Just a handful of fur, four clinging thistledown paws, and a heart beating under Anda's thumb. Its face was like a pansy. Black and white, and velvety and wistful. As soon as Anda had it snuggled in her arms, she wanted it.

"Bella, I'll call you! After the church bells!" she whispered. "And you're going to stay with me! You *dear* little thing."

She tucked the kitten inside her track suit top and pulled the zipper up.

"Who do you think you are? Wonder Woman?"

The man's voice startled Anda. She swung round, and there was a fireman on a long ladder coming up the roof.

4

Down below was the fire engine, throbbing away in the road, its blue light twisting through the trees. More and more people had gathered, some of them people Anda knew. And kids she knew from the village school. She was surprised. She waved and shouted.

"Got the kitten!"

But nobody cheered. Probably they were all cross with her. The grown-ups would be, anyway!

"Hang on to me. We'll soon get you down!" said the fireman.

"But I can climb down! I'm quite all right!" said Anda. She stared at his helmet. "Why have you got that on? There isn't a fire!"

The man shrugged.

"Regulations," he said.

To Anda's annoyance he reached out and picked her up, kitten and all.

"Put your arms round my neck and hold tight!"

"But I can climb down!"

The fireman wouldn't listen. He held Anda tightly as he climbed down the ladder. She had no choice but to hold on! Inside her track suit the kitten was crawling about. She could feel it trying to burrow its head out through her collar.

Within minutes they were on the ground.

"You silly, silly little girl! You might have been killed!"

Anda looked up at the man from the village Post Office. His face was the color of a dish of rhubarb.

"What are your parents doing, letting you up there?" he thundered. "Don't they care?"

Anda's brown eyes sparkled angrily.

"They *do* care!" she said, looking him straight in the eye. "And they know where I am. I went to mail a letter for Dad!"

She looked round at all the faces. They were all staring at her and Anda hated that.

The fireman patted Anda on the head. "I think she's a brave little girl! Now, where's that kitten?"

Anda grinned. She undid her zipper and a little face appeared.

"Aw!" said everyone.

Someone reached out to pick up the kitten, but it clung to Anda furiously, its needlelike claws entangled in her shirt. She put a hand over it protectively. Little Bella. Bella would be her kitten now!

"It comes from Holly Cottage. Mrs. Wood. She's got kittens."

"Bet you'd like to keep him, wouldn't you?" said the fireman kindly.

Anda nodded. She swallowed. To knock on Mrs. Wood's door was worse than climbing the roof. Anda didn't like Mrs. Wood. Once she had caught

Anda balance-walking along her garden wall and given her a telling off that had echoed all down the village street, and Anda had walked away with a very red face. Mrs. Wood was not likely to give Anda one of her kittens after that!

"Come on, I'll take you," said the kind fireman.

Anda and the fireman and the kitten knocked on the door of Holly Cottage. And to Anda's surprise Mrs. Wood actually smiled.

She reached out a bony hand and plucked Bella away from the girl's shoulder.

"We've had a litter of six. They're all over the place! Come and see!" She opened a door and led them into a dark room full of plants and heavy curtains. "This is the Mum cat," she said, pointing to a basket in the corner.

She put Bella down and the kitten scampered across to its mother. There was much meowing and nuzzling and licking.

"Do you want homes for them?" asked the fireman.

"Oh yes. Some of them are booked already. Of course, I can't go out much, you see. My arthritis."

They chatted on about cats and dogs and geraniums, while Anda tried to find a moment to ask if Bella had a home. But suddenly she found herself walking back down the path and the fire-

7

man was saying good-bye. She hadn't found the courage to ask about Bella!

Anda was brave enough for anything, except knocking on Mrs. Wood's door! And now beautiful little Bella was shut away inside Holly Cottage.

2

Olympic Gymnasts

Home was a mile out of the village, up a steep lane that got stonier and stonier as it climbed between high banks. The track branched off, one path going up to the heather-covered moor where sheep and ponies grazed, the other dipping down along the hillside to some birch trees. There stood Hooty Cottage. A real shambles, Anda's gran called it. Old sheds and bits of tin and chickens everywhere!

She didn't bother opening the gate but shinnied up the chicken house, rolled across the roof, and landed with a mighty leap in the garden.

"Anda!" Her dad was standing right there, tying up the bean canes. "Can't you arrive home in a civilized manner?"

He wasn't really cross. If he was cross his beard would bristle and his eyes would go pebbly. Most of the time he was peaceful and twinkly. Anda adored him. At school she would fight anyone who said, "Your dad's a hippie."

"I mailed your letter!" she said, hanging round his waist.

"Good girl!"

He went on tying string round the bean canes. He was a tall man with a wild frizz of sandy-colored hair and a gingery beard. He wore denim shorts and sandals and a tartan shirt.

"See anyone?" he asked Anda.

"Dad, there was this kitten. And it couldn't get down, so — "

"So you rescued it!" he said, laughing. "Trust you. Where was it? Up a tree?"

"It was only on the church roof, Daddy. I went up the pipe and across and round the bell tower and then this fireman came and carried me down. It was a darling little kitten and it belongs — "

"What?" Her dad gave her a roar loud enough to rock the chicken house. "You WHAT?"

"Went up the pipe and — "

"You climbed on the church roof? And the fire department got you down?"

"Well, no. Well, they came to get the kitten really, but I got it first. I thought it would get wet. I could have climbed down okay, but. . . . "

Bill squatted down and put his two bean-stained hands on Anda's shoulders. His face was serious.

10

"Tell me that again, slowly," he said. "Tell me exactly what you did."

Anda began to feel that she'd done something dreadful from the look on his face. She explained as slowly as she could.

Bill seemed caught between grinning and being angry. In the end he roared with laughter. Then he frowned again.

"But you mustn't do things like that, Anda."

"What's she done now?"

Anda's mum was coming down the path with two buckets, on her way to milk the goats. She was small and pretty, with a face exactly like Anda's, except for its long, stringy hair. She never wore a dress. Always jeans. Sometimes Anda wished she would wear a pretty dress. Her mum was sweet and gentle sometimes, but more often tired and disheveled. She was stricter with Anda than Bill.

"Oh no! Anda! You might have been killed!" she cried when she heard what Anda had done.

"It was okay, Mum. Why does everyone make such a fuss?" said Anda. "Everyone was shouting at me to get down."

"I don't care about *them*! It's *you* I'm concerned about," stormed her mother, her voice building up to a squeak. "Anda! You *are not* to climb things!"

"Oh, don't go on at her, Lynne!" said Bill, seeing

Anda's face going pale. "It's the way she is!"

"Well, I can't cope with her!" raved her mother. "She knows she shouldn't do it! And you don't stop her! Well, if you don't, I will. Go indoors, Anda."

Anda went, dragging her feet, leaving her parents arguing in the beans. No chance of her having Bella now! It really wasn't fair! Why couldn't people be pleased because she had climbed the church roof to rescue a kitten?

"Look what she's done in the first week of vacation!" her mum was screeching in the beans. "She's written off a pair of shoes in the stream, she's broken the barn door swinging on it, split the corn sacks jumping on them, and countless other things. I mean, how can one child be so destructive?"

"She's got too much energy, I guess. She doesn't mean to be destructive, Lynne." Good old dad. He was defending her again!

"And look at the seat of your jeans!" exclaimed her mother, coming in at the door.

Anda twisted to look at the blackened seat of her jeans.

"That's from sliding down the church roof," she explained, and without warning the tears came burning and boiling down her cheeks. "Why can't you be pleased with me, Mum? I climbed up the church roof to get Bella and the fireman said I was brave anyway. You're cross with me all the time. You don't like me. You don't like me. You don't!"

"Oh Anda!" Lynne held out her arms and held the stormy little girl tightly. "Of course we like you, darling! It's just that you get yourself into so much mischief."

"But I don't mean to," Anda sobbed. She didn't cry often. When she did she couldn't stop.

Her mother sighed. "I don't know what to do with you. I really don't."

"You won't really shut me indoors?"

"No, of course not! But just do try not to be always climbing things and breaking things!"

That made Anda cry even more. She blurted it all out, about wanting the kitten and being afraid to knock on Mrs. Wood's door!

Lynne was not very hopeful. "I don't think we'd dare have a cat, not with all the chickens!" she said. "Anyway, we'll see. I'll talk to Daddy. You go and do something positive, Anda, for goodness' sake. Do you want to do the pots or milk the goats?"

Anda looked at the pile of dishes in the sink.

"I'll milk the goats," she said.

She dried her face on her sleeve and took the two buckets awkwardly, one on each arm. She loved the two goats, Millie and Mollie. She put her arms round Millie's black and white neck and told the goat her troubles. Millie listened attentively, flicking her curved ears backward and forward, and blinking her gold eyes.

Milking the goats was easy, once you got the hang of it. She watched the jets of creamy milk filling the bucket, and tried to stop crying. It was her tenth birthday in two weeks. Maybe her parents would let her have Bella then!

But before that, something happened that changed Anda's life completely!

She was having tea at Gran's when it happened. It was a Saturday and Gran had taken her shopping and bought some cream cakes for tea. She'd bought Anda an adventure book.

"To keep you quiet," Gran said.

Gran lived in a bungalow in the new housing development in Elmsford. The big attraction at Gran's for Anda was the color TV, which was always switched on. Anda didn't have a television at all, so she always wanted to watch it, no matter what was on; the bright colors fascinated her.

Anda knew she had to sit still at Gran's. No swinging from doors or rolling on the floor! Today she tried extra hard to sit and read her new book.

But suddenly something on the television caught her attention. A girl was flying through the air, like a swallow! She landed and stood with her arms stretched high. Then she smiled, waved with both hands, and ran off to the sound of cheering. Anda sat up straight, her eyes glued to the screen.

Next they showed another girl dancing and tumbling to music on a huge square mat. She danced and leaped and did the fastest handsprings. She turned somersaults in the air. Things Anda thought only circus acrobats did!

"A marvelous performance," raved the commentator. "And this little girl is only fifteen years old!"

The girl waved to the cheering crowds in the Olympic stadium. She wore a white leotard and ballet-type shoes, and her hair was tied in a ponytail with a white ribbon.

Anda caught her breath. A spark of an idea burned in her mind.

Other girls from different countries came on the screen. All of them were graceful and agile. They performed on a balance beam and swung on some high bars.

Anda jumped up and ran into the kitchen.

"Gran! Gran!"

"For goodness' sake, Anda!" Gran rattled the tea cups.

"Gran, look! Look at these girls. Quick! Quick!"

Gran bustled into the living room, surprised at

the look of intensity on Anda's face. Together they watched a little Russian girl on the beam.

"Oh yes," said Gran. "I love to watch the gymnastics!"

"Gymnastics?" repeated Anda, tasting the word for the first time. At school they did PE or Music and Movement, both of which she enjoyed, but never anything quite like that! In herself Anda knew that she could do some of the things the Olympic girls were doing!

"I could do that!" she said excitedly.

"Go on!" teased Gran. "You'd tie yourself in a knot!"

"But I could, Gran! If I practiced and practiced, and then I could go in the Olympics when I'm older!"

"No, Anda. . . . You don't understand," said Gran. "Those girls are specially trained with special facilities. You couldn't do that in Elmsford!"

Anda's face fell.

"But I can do handstands and — "

"No, don't show me!" said Gran, restraining her. "We're going to have tea now. Anyway, I've seen you doing handstands before."

"But I can do something else, too. I could do it on the lawn!"

"No," said Gran. "It's teatime. And I don't think

the neighbors would like a display of your underpants, thank you."

Anda sighed. She had a dress on today, white socks, and pretty sandals, all of which were kept just for visiting Gran. She couldn't wait to get home now and put on her jeans and do gymnastics on the lawn. So she ate as fast as she could, and Gran looked at her disapprovingly.

"You're very quiet, Anda!" she remarked as she drove her home in her neat blue car.

But Anda's mind was miles away. In her head she was seeing again the girl in the white leotard, and the Russian girl on the beam. And she was seeing herself doing it.

"She's got her head full of those Olympic gymnasts!" warned Gran when they got to the cottage. "I can't get any sense out of her! Or into her!"

"I'm going to change into my PE things from school," said Anda and she charged upstairs, leaving her parents podding a mountain of peas.

Her PE things — red shorts and a T-shirt and black sneakers — were still in their bag in the corner where she had chucked them on the last day of term.

She changed quickly, throwing her dress and her posh sandals up to hit the ceiling. At the top of the stairs she stopped. An interesting conversation was going on, and she could hear bits of it.

"Perhaps there's a gymnastics club! There's bound to be one in town — at the Sports Center."

"I'll inquire."

"Shh," said Anda's dad, and after that she only heard whispers. She thought she heard the words *birthday* and *gymnastics*. Then she heard the word *kitten* quite distinctly! Her birthday was next Friday. She would be ten. What were they planning?

She chose that moment to run downstairs and jump the last three steps.

"No, no, Anda! You're not to wear those in the holidays. You'll have nothing for school!" moaned Lynne. "Go and change. And I'll bet you've left your dress in a heap. Go and hang it up. Then you can help pod the peas!"

Anda turned on her heel. She didn't dare groan in front of Gran! She raced upstairs and did an angry somersault on her bed. She fell off on the floor and it shook the whole cottage.

"What on earth are you doing?"

Anda stood rubbing her elbow where she'd banged it. It seemed she couldn't do anything right!

3
Handstands

"**B**oots off and happy birthday in that order!" said Gran.

Mud was not allowed in Gran's house. Bill and Anda stepped out of their tall rubber boots. Bill winked at Anda.

"My socks are horrible," he said.

"I don't wish to know that, thank you!" said Gran brightly. "Have you got the — "

"Shh! No. Not yet!" Bill put his finger to his lips.

"Doesn't she know?" mouthed Gran.

"I heard you!" giggled Anda.

"You mean about the thousand-and-one-piece jigsaw we're giving her?" said Bill in a loud voice. Anda couldn't bear jigsaws.

"He's been teasing me all the way!" cried Anda, looking expectantly at Gran. Gran had a beautiful blue-green dress on and a big silver pendant. Her ash-blonde hair was swept into elaborate waves.

It was difficult to believe she was Bill's mum!

She took Anda into the kitchen.

"Oh Gran!"

"Hey, that's really wow!" exclaimed Bill.

A fantastic cake stood on the table. In the middle Gran had done a picture in colored icing of a girl gymnast. Her leotard was pink icing and it had ANDA written across it.

"That has to be a good luck cake!" said Bill.

"It's wonderful, Gran. How did you do it?"

Gran swelled with pride. "Look underneath, Anda. There's something else!"

She lifted the silver dish revealing an envelope.

"A card! Oh thanks, Gran."

Inside the card was a green ticket. It said FERNDALE OLYMPIC GYMNASTICS CLUB. MEMBERSHIP CARD. ANDA BARNES.

"Gymnastics Club?" squealed Anda.

"It's at Ferndale School. And you can go on Monday at four o'clock," explained Gran. "I joined you up for six months to see if you like it. They train all through their vacation. It looked well-organized. I went and had a look. There's children there even younger than you!"

"Wow!" Anda's eyes were sparkling. Monday at four o'clock. Mentally she worked it out. Four whole days and three nights to wait!

"But the instructor — a lady it was I spoke to,

said it was hard work!" warned Gran. "You have to work really hard, and do what you're told."

"Hoorah!" cheered Bill.

"How did you know about the club, Gran?" asked Anda, thinking that Gran had probably never turned a somersault in her life.

"I didn't know, dear," Gran explained, plugging in the kettle. "I went to the library and asked."

"The library!"

"Oh yes. You can find out anything you want to know if you ask!" said Gran.

Gran and Bill sat chatting over coffee. Anda sat and gazed at the cake and dreamed about being a gymnast while the rain lashed savagely at the window and Gran's garden whirled and tossed.

"Come on then, Anda. Surprise number two!" said Bill.

They left in boots and raincoats. The old van, Murgatroyd, wouldn't start. Bill sat there turning the key again and again. "Blast the thing!"

Anda was used to Murgatroyd's not-starting music. She sat curled up on its front seat, reading the blurb on the back of her club card. She had another card with it. It said BRITISH AMATEUR GYMNASTICS ASSOCIATION. PERSONAL ACHIEVEMENT CARD. AWARD 4. Inside was a list of ten things you were supposed to be able to do. She didn't understand what all of them were exactly, but she knew one or two that they had done at school. Bridge — she could do that! Handstand — yes, she could even walk on her hands. Headstand — she could do that!

"What's a forward roll, Daddy?" she asked.

Murgatroyd started at last and they rattled away.

"A fifty-mile-an-hour jet-propelled sausage!" Bill said. Surprise number two was not going to be much, he added, when she had stopped giggling. "We can't give you things that cost a lot of money, Anda," he said, glancing at her. "We're trying to be self-sufficient, you know that, don't you?"

"Yes."

Bill only worked part-time as a bricklayer. That paid for the essentials. But apart from that, they tried to grow all their own food and manage without posh furniture. Anda knew that because it had been explained to her many times. It was the only way they could stay in the cottage.

Her parents loved Hooty Combe very much. And so did Anda. She loved the primroses in spring, the long-haired sheep that ran wild with their baby lambs, the gray squirrels in the wood, and the great silver gulls that blew in from the sea. She loved the winter when the snow blew sideways, and the summer when she played for hours by the stream and went to bed to the sound of the hooting owls that gave Hooty Combe its name.

When Murgatroyd stopped outside Holly Cottage she couldn't believe it. She stared at Bill over a big smile. "Are we having Bella? Are we?"

Bill ruffled the tuft of hair that stuck up over Anda's forehead. "It might be one of the other kittens. It depends whether Bella's already booked or not. You won't mind terribly, will you?"

"No," said Anda dubiously.

Mrs. Wood led them into the room with the heavy curtains. "It's a little she-cat, you know. That's why she wasn't chosen. They all want tom-cats."

Bella was nowhere to be seen. Mrs. Wood looked under the chairs and behind the curtains and on the bookshelves.

"She's not been outside much. Not since that day she climbed the roof! Now wherever is she?"

"I can see her!" squealed Anda, pointing to one of the chairs. A moving bump was going up the back of the chair, under the cover.

Mrs. Wood grumbled while she extracted Bella from the chair. The kitten emerged flat-eared and wild-eyed in her hand. "Wretched animals!" she said. "Here you are. Hold on to her."

She dumped the wild black and white bundle in Anda's lap. The kitten was a bit bigger, but she still weighed hardly anything. Suddenly the tiny face looked up at Anda with eyes like blue jewels.

"Hello!" said Anda. Bella stared at her, head on one side. Then she crawled up Anda's chest, right up to her face. She touched noses with Anda. White whiskers tickled her face, and the kitten drew back and sat looking. Then she put out a paw and dabbed at the string from Anda's parka.

"Oh, isn't she darling! Isn't she tiny!" breathed Anda. In her arms the kitten began to purr as if she knew she had found a home.

"Cats know," said Mrs. Wood. "She picked you out!"

"Won't she miss her mother?" asked Anda.

"She's eight weeks. She can lap all right. But only give her tiny meals," said Mrs. Wood.

"What do we owe you?" Bill asked, putting out a finger to rub Bella's ear. "Isn't she beautiful!"

"Nothing. I'm glad to find homes for them. Anyway, it'll cost you enough to have her injected against cat flu and all that."

"Injected?" said Anda, horrified.

"There you are!" said Bill. "I said you were getting an injection for your birthday!"

"And the price of cat food!"

"Anyway, thanks a lot, Mrs. Wood. We must be going."

"Thanks," said Anda.

They left Mrs. Wood grumbling about the price of everything. Murgatroyd's noisy engine had no effect on Bella, and she curled up happily on Anda's lap, patting and playing. Anda couldn't stop gazing at her, and kept up a stream of exclamations.

"Oh look, Daddy! She's got pink feet! Her paws are pink on the bottom. Like pink beads!

"Look at her white whiskers! Oh, she's got little white eyelashes! Why are her eyes blue?"

"They'll change," said Bill, steering Murgatroyd carefully round a group of moorland sheep. "They'll go green as she gets older. Or yellow. Oh, she's magic, isn't she!"

"This is the superest birthday ever!" said Anda with a happy sigh.

"Make the most of it," said Bill.

All that weekend the rain poured and the wind blew. Bill and Lynne rushed about in raincoats and boots, tying and staking their precious plants against the wind. Anda sat podding peas for hours, and Bella had a marvelous time chasing the stray ones around the floor. When the kitten finally climbed into her cardboard box to sleep, Anda went to the barn to practice gymnastics.

The barn floor was cold and gritty, but it didn't matter! As long as she kept away from the corn sacks! She spread some of the empty ones out on the floor for mats, and made one nice thick pile to practice headstands on.

Anda had always been able to stand on her head. And do cartwheels. Her teacher said she did lovely cartwheels. So she practiced those, too. But mostly she practiced handstands. She could lean over backward and make a bridge. That was something she was always being asked to do at school!

She felt sure she would surprise everyone at the gymnastics club!

4

To Be a Gymnast

Anda stood miserably at the door of the gym-nasium, watching the track-suited children who were running about putting out mats and benches. She wasn't frightened of the gymnastics, but paralyzed by an illogical fear of walking into a crowd of strangers.

At the last minute she'd pleaded with Lynne. "Please take me in. I can't go on my own."

"Rubbish. It'll be good for you." And Lynne had driven determinedly away in Murgatroyd.

Two girls swept past her, through the swing doors, laughing and talking. They ignored Anda. Her throat full of panicky tears, she crept back to the changing room.

And then she saw Julienne.

Julienne was struggling into a blue leotard, her clothes spread around her on the floor.

"Oh, I hate this horrible leotard!" she was

27

grumbling. "It makes me prickle. The trouble is. . . . "

Anda stood, wondering how anyone could find so much to say to a complete stranger! For a gymnast Julienne was heavily built. Her moon-pale face between two chunky brown braids had a worried look. It was not a happy face, but when she smiled at Anda her eyes were blueberry blue and friendly.

"Are you just starting today?" she asked.

"Yes," said Anda.

"Haven't you got a leotard?"

"No."

"It doesn't matter. But you'll have to take those off," advised Julienne, pointing to Anda's black sneakers. "I'm Julienne Wellington. Hello!"

"Hello. I'm Anda Barnes."

"How old?"

"Ten."

"Me, too. Where are you from?"

"Elmsford." Anda took off her sneakers and socks.

"I'll look after you."

Julienne talked incessantly. Anda followed her about, wide-eyed and silent.

The enormous gymnasium was well-equipped. Wall bars. Ropes. Benches and beams. Asymmetric bars. And a huge trampoline!

"We aren't allowed on that!" said Julienne, seeing Anda's eyes light up. "We have to have spotters!"

Before Anda could ask what spotters were, Julienne had sprinted over to a trolley piled high with blue mats.

"Tumbling mats," she explained. "We have to put them all out."

As more and more children arrived, Anda felt painfully aware that she was the only one in shorts and a T-shirt.

"Julienne," she said as they undid the straps from one of the blue mats, "what's a forward roll?"

Julienne and another girl looked at each other and laughed.

"Don't you even know that?" shrieked the other girl, a blonde, ponytailed, pixie-faced child. "That's the easiest thing!" Anda took an instant dislike to her. She came and undid the strap Anda was undoing, impatiently with efficient pink fingers. "Not like that! Like this!"

"That's Lena," Julienne said. "And that's Christie over there. She's our instructor. And that's John. He's her husband."

Bewildered, Anda followed Julienne to where a track-suited woman was sitting, surrounded by piles of paper, little heaps of money, and a tangle of wires coming from a tape recorder. A group of girls stood round her saying "Where's my . . . "

and "Can I. . . . " Christie was coping patiently, her wavy gray-haired head bent over a chart.

Despite the gray hair her face was young, and when she saw Anda it broke into a magical smile. Straightaway Anda felt welcome.

"You must be Anda!"

Christie didn't say Anda Barnes, like they did at school.

"You can call me Christie, okay?"

"Okay," Anda smiled. "I couldn't wait for today! I want to go to the Olympics!"

The other girls giggled, and Julienne rolled her eyes comically. But Christie looked at her solemnly.

"Right! We'd better get started then, hadn't we. Got your card? Lovely. Good girl," she said, taking it. "You can go with Group D, that's our beginners' group, and stay with them."

"Okay," said Anda.

Christie put a hand on Anda's shoulder.

"I'll just say this to you, Anda, before we begin. Don't go on any apparatus unless you've been told to, and don't do anything until after the warm-up. You don't understand what that is, do you?"

"No."

"Well, it's very important. Even Olympic gymnasts still have to do it. Try to copy the exercises the others are doing. The secret is to practice every day at home."

"Oh I do," said Anda, and Christie laughed softly.

The group consisted of two five-year-olds, one fragile dark-skinned girl called Elizabeth, and several who looked about ten. One of them, with a pale freckled face, looked scruffier than the others in faded training tights and a scruffy sweater. She looked tough and alone. Anda stood by her and asked her name.

"Kerry."

Christie started the tape recorder. In three groups the forty girls in the gym began to move. Anda stood for a moment, fascinated.

Left behind, and seeing Christie looking at her, she joined in. First they were running on their toes. Then leaping sideways. Bending and stretching followed, touching the floor, and swinging.

Next it was bridges. Down flat, then up, with backs arched.

"Try to get your legs straight!"

Christie went around helping. She passed Anda who looked at her anxiously, upside down.

"Good," she said. "You're all right."

More exercises followed. Anda thought she would never remember them all! Some were difficult, especially one that involved sitting with legs wide apart and getting your chest on the floor. And the splits were difficult. Nobody in her group could do it. Except for Kerry.

"It takes months!" Christie said. "Don't force it. Let your muscles get used to it!"

By the time the warm-up was finished, Anda felt friends with the group.

"We're beginning with floor," Christie said. "Start with forward rolls!"

At last she was to discover what those were! Anda positioned herself at the back of the line to watch.

"Oh, somersaults!" she thought when she saw the others rolling over and over. "I can do *those*!"

So she rolled at speed along the mat, three times, hoping to impress Christie. The girl in front turned round angrily as Anda crashed into her. "Watch out."

"Come here, Anda."

She went to Christie.

"Watch," said Christie. "Watch Lena."

She called Lena over and asked her to do a forward roll. With a contemptuous glance at Anda, Lena stretched tall, stood poised, and then sprang into a graceful roll.

"Did her head touch the floor?" asked Christie.

"No."

"What did her legs do?"

"I don't know."

"Watch again."

Patiently she made Lena repeat the roll several times so that Anda could watch.

"Now you try."

Anda suddenly found she didn't know how to begin! Christie showed her how to squat and spring. Remembering to tuck her head in and to get up without using her hands was more difficult than she'd thought! Christie wanted her to keep her ankles and knees together as well. Over and over again she tried.

Backward rolls were even more complicated! Anda decided to practice the two rolls at home. She hadn't expected to fail at something so easy.

Handstands next. Then headstands. She wasn't doing those right, either!

"It's our turn for beam now," said Christie.

There were three beams, one at floor level, one at knee height, and the high full-sized "Continental Sports" beam. Anda couldn't wait. She bounded and skipped.

"Can I go on the big one?" she asked Christie.

"Yes, okay," said Christie. "Just try it out. Get the feel of it. Walk about on it and sit on it. We'll teach you some things to do when you're used to it! No, Kerry, let Anda have a minute to herself first. You work on the benches."

Kerry got down, her face expressionless.

"What are you staring at?" she said to Anda.

"Nothing."

Kerry turned her back. Something was wrong with her, Anda thought, puzzled.

At shoulder height, the big beam was no higher for Anda than many of the gates and walls she had climbed! Under her bare feet it was hard, velvety, and high in the air! It felt marvelous. She walked straight to the other end, turned, and ran back. Christie was standing close, her face anxious and surprised.

From watching the Olympic girls on television, Anda thought she had to dance on the beam. So she danced, stretching and twisting. It took concentration, and a lot of inelegant wobbling.

"John!" Christie was shouting.

John came quickly and stood beside Christie.

"Look at this child!" said Christie.

Together they watched Anda as she danced, with her birdlike face and flexible toes. Her balance was steady, her movements, though untrained, were graceful as she moved through a fantasy world of her own, small and strong and sunbrowned. She decided recklessly to try a cart-wheel.

"No, Anda!"

Too late!

Simultaneously Christie and John ran sideways and caught Anda as she came flying off the end of the beam.

"Can I go back up?" she laughed.

John and Christie stared at each other. They didn't tell Anda that most children on the beam for the first time just walked gingerly along it. Some found it scary.

"Have you been on an Olympic beam before? Or any beam?" asked John curiously.

"No. Only an old fence post in the garden," said Anda. "Can I go back up?"

"Yes, for a few minutes. But *no* cartwheels or handstands. Just dance, okay?"

"Okay," said Anda. But later on she got a quiet lecture from Christie about safety. And Julienne told her in no uncertain terms as well.

"You're nuts! You must be nuts! Imagine doing a cartwheel your first time on the beam! You're crazy! You'll get chucked out of the gym club if you take silly risks! Christie won't have that!"

"But I didn't know. I thought I could do one!" protested Anda.

The vault was strange to Anda.

Watching Julienne's group finish their turn at vaulting, she thought it looked easy, especially with a spring board, or reuther board, as it was called. Open-mouthed, she watched Lena sprinting past. Bang, off the reuther board, up into a handstand, and over.

"Have I got to do that?" asked Anda, looking at Christie.

"No way!" said Christie. "You'll just be squatting your feet on and jumping off to start with!"

Julienne came next. But she chickened, running then stopping with her arms over the vaulting buck.

"We haven't got time for chickening!" John said to her.

Julienne rolled her eyes comically and returned for a second go. Her last chance, John said.

Julienne didn't do a handspring vault like Lena. She managed a sort of scramble, caught her foot on the buck, and fell.

"Don't *worry* about it, Julienne," said Christie kindly.

Julienne managed a smile, but her distress was obvious.

"You have to be tough to be a gymnast!" said Christie. Then she looked at Kerry. "You aren't vaulting, Kerry, are you?"

"No," said Kerry in her quiet voice.

"You go and do floor work," said Christie. "Gently. No somies."

Kerry turned on her heel. She looked upset, too! That was one major thing Anda learned in her first lesson. That gymnastics was not all laughter and cartwheels! There were tears there, too, in the gym.

When her turn came, Anda ran confidently and bounced on to the reuther board. But it was not as springy as she'd expected! Slam, she hit the buck with her stomach and would have fallen back if Christie hadn't caught her.

"I could do it better than that!"

Cross with herself, she had another try.

"Really tuck your knees up high this time," advised Christie.

But it took several more crashes before Anda managed to get her feet on the buck and stand up.

John was watching her.

"Let me have her for five minutes," he said to Christie. "Can you watch my girls beam?"

John gave Anda so many instructions that her head felt like a computer! Chin up, knees up, run fast, run slow, push with your arms, land on the right bit of the spring board, stop when you land! John wanted her to do a through vault. She ran like a tiger, hurting her feet as she stamped on the reuther board.

The result was a breathtaking jump, through her arms and onto the crash mat.

"Stop when you land! Straight back!"

He steadied her.

"Great!" he said. "Now take it again!"

Anda ran back.

"Wow!" she said to Elizabeth. "I didn't know I could do that."

"I'll bet you don't do it next time!" laughed Elizabeth.

Anda was thinking the same. John wagged a finger at her.

"Think, think, *think*!" he called.

She did. Focusing her attention on the buck and John's instructions, she ran, and flew over, this time with her feet tucked up neatly. Stopping took a lot of effort, but she managed it, and stood with a straight back and raised arms.

"Good girl!" said John, and again he asked her, "Have you done any vaulting before, Anda?"

"A bit. But our vaulting box at school isn't so high."

"Oh," said John. "A little village school, is it?"

"Yes. Elmsford."

"I know," said John. He beamed down at Anda.

Here at last was the talent he had dreamed of finding! For ten years he and Christie had run Ferndale Olympic Gymnastic Club. Their girls had entered competitions, gained a few medals, passed lots of grades. But Ferndale had never yet had a champion!

John kept his thoughts to himself. After all, Anda might not stick with the rigorous training.

"Now don't go trying that at home, will you?" he said. "Only in the gym with proper equipment and someone to catch you! That's really important, Anda. Are you listening?"

"Yes."

"See you next week, then? Go on, your group is on the bars now!"

After the club Julienne was eager to talk to Anda.

"You did okay, didn't you? First time!" she said enthusiastically.

"I don't know," said Anda.

"Except for your nutty cartwheel on the beam!" cried Julienne. She turned to Lena who was putting her clothes away in a neat white bag. "Did you see what this mad fool did on the beam?" she shrieked. "She only did a cartwheel and went flying!"

Lena looked curiously at Anda.

39

"I'll bet you got a lecture from John!" she said.

"Yes. And one from Christie," said Anda, embarrassed.

Kerry was there with Lena, her face puffed and upset. The two girls were friends. Lena put her arm round Kerry and they walked off together.

"What's the matter with Kerry?" asked Anda.

"Oh, Kerry!" said Julienne. "She's not really like that. She used to train with the competition girls and then she got sick. She had an operation and she's been in the hospital for months and months. Now she can't train properly for about a year. That's why she's upset all the time."

Anda felt sorry for Kerry.

She and Julienne wandered outside to wait for their mothers. Anda told Julienne about Bella, and Hooty Cottage, and the stream.

"You lucky *thing*," said Julienne. "I'm not allowed any pets. We live in an apartment. Just Mum and me. She and my dad are divorced."

"You'll have to come up one day. We could do gymnastics on the lawn. And jump the Hooty Stream," said Anda generously.

"I'd love to. Could I?" Julienne's eyes shone.

Julienne's mum arrived in a gleaming car. She wore a stylish suit, makeup, and had all the windows shut. She smiled icily at Anda.

A moment later Lynne drove up in muddy,

spluttering Murgatroyd, her hair flying and all the door handles tied up with string.

"How was it?" she asked.

"Fabulous!" said Anda.

"You didn't make a fool of yourself, then!"

"No!" Anda looked at Julienne and grinned. "Well — not quite!"

Julienne rolled her eyes and said teasingly, "Cartwheels?"

Anda grinned and waved as Julienne was whisked away in the sleek car. "See you next week!"

5

You Can't Go!

Anda flung herself on her bed and cried. The rough blankets burned her cheeks, and the walls shook with her sobs.

"You can't go. So accept it!" Lynne's voice called upstairs.

Outside, the autumn day was toasted and still. A thousand leaves fell silently in the Hooty glen. The four o'clock November sun was sinking. Through her tears pink light shone into her room with its messy floor and white walls covered in posters of gymnasts. Five past four. Ten past four. Warm-up would be starting now! Where's Anda? Why isn't she here? And today she was due to complete her fourth British Amateur Gymnastics Association Award, Grade 1.

Determined to catch up with Julienne, she had worked every day at her exercises until she hurt. Horrified to hear of her using sacks in the barn,

Christie had lent her a faded tumbling mat so that she could safely practice her agilities. When sunny, she worked on the level turf by the Hooty Stream, sometimes staying there until dark.

She had flown through Award 4 and 3. Award 2 had taken longer. The backroll to handstand was particularly difficult. Anda thought her arms would never be strong enough!

The four BAGA Awards, Christie told her, were only the first step. After that, she would be invited for extra training with the "competition squad." And that had become her burning ambition.

Gymnastics had given her something to work and dream for. She knew that John and Christie thought her talented and expected great things of her. But today was the second dreadful time she had missed going to the club!

"You'll get thrown out if you don't come every week!" Julienne had joked, but the words rang in Anda's head. She and Julienne had become close friends, although Julienne was a bit jealous of Anda's fast progress.

"Where were you last week?" Christie had said, while John looked at her coldly.

"We had a sick goat," explained Anda. "And Mummy had to wait in for the vet." She hadn't minded so much that time because of her concern for poor Millie. She'd stayed in the goat shed stroking, soothing the distressed goat until the vet had arrived.

Tonight it was different. Murgatroyd wouldn't start. So there she was, stuck! And Lynne's casual attitude about it enraged Anda to the point of tears. She wanted to kick Murgatroyd to pieces! Anything to stop Lynne going on about her housework in her calm infuriating way!

Eventually Lynne came upstairs bringing tea and biscuits. Bella was on her shoulder.

"Come on, love. You can't stay like this forever," she said, gently putting Bella down on the bed. Bella was almost a cat now, fluffy and adorable and very, very naughty! Butting her head against Anda's cheek, she purred loudly, walking round and round Anda's head until she sat up.

"Dear little cat!" murmured Anda, cuddling her. "She cares, anyway!"

"That's not necessary, Anda," said Lynne, tight-faced. "You're a horrible child sometimes. You really are. I have feelings, too! Do you think I liked it, Murgatroyd not starting? Do you?"

Anda shrugged.

"You aren't the only important person in the world!" said Lynne. "If Murgatroyd needs a new battery, it means that Daddy's got to take on extra work when he's already worn out keeping this place going! He's just as important as you! And what if you don't go to the stupid gym club for once?"

She leaned her arms on the window, staring out at the pink sky.

"Tonight was special, Mummy. You don't understand," sniffed Anda. She held the hot tea mug and sipped it noisily.

"Why don't I understand?" asked Lynne wearily. But when Anda tried to explain how Christie and John felt about her being talented and joining the competition girls, Lynne just said:

"Don't you think you're stretching it a bit, Anda? You're far too young for competitions! I know you're good at it, love, and I know you've practiced, but it's only for fun, surely! You're too young to be taking it that seriously!"

This enraged Anda even more.

"But I'm *not*, Mummy! If anything, I'm too old! John says I started a bit late, that's why I've had to work so hard! Honestly, Mummy, if you knew! Spider Girl's only *seven* and she trains with the competition girls!"

"Just what is it going to involve — this competition training?" asked Lynne.

"It means I can go on Thursday nights as well. And Saturday mornings if I want to. You don't have to pay!"

"But Anda, we *can't* take you three times a week!" exploded Lynne. "The time, and the gas, and the hanging about in town waiting for you! You can forget that! I'm telling you!"

There was a thunderous silence.

Bella went on relentlessly pouncing on bits of the bedspread.

One by one Anda's dreams flew out of the window. Hatred gripped her throat and she turned on Lynne who stood at the window blocking the light.

"You can't stop me from going!" Her voice came out squeaky and strange.

Lynne stood her ground. "Can't I?"

And of course she could!

"I'll run away then."

"There's the door!" said Lynne.

"You're horrid!" said Anda, turning in the open doorway. "And I *hate* you!"

Later she was to remember with guilt Lynne's shattered white face looking at her.

Down the stairs she thundered, through the cabbage-strewn kitchen, and out. Bella streaked after her, back arched, tail kinked.

Left alone in the cottage, Lynne sat down on Anda's bed and covered her face with her long thin hands.

"Cool it, cool it," she kept telling herself. Anda

had run away before. She would be back!

But Anda, as she ran along the banks of the Hooty Stream and up through the crunching bracken, was determined. She would never go back. Never. She climbed on and on up the twisting path, right to the top of the moors. The sky shone overhead like a china bowl, blue and pink at the edges.

A white obelisk stood on the summit. Anda sat on it, kicking it with her track shoes. Below her the lights of Elmsford twinkled through the trees. She could hear sheep baa-ing, and the distant bubbling of the Hooty Stream.

A loud wail reached her ears.

"Bella!"

Surely Bella hadn't followed her right up there! The half-grown kitten crept out of the bracken, looking absolutely terrified. She had never been so far from the cottage before.

"Oh, poor Bella."

Although Anda picked her up, Bella would not be calmed.

"I'll have to take you home!"

Reluctantly she set off down the path. Bella wouldn't be carried but ran ahead of Anda in kink-tailed gallops. Within sight of home, the kitten relaxed and started to chase leaves. Anda sat up in the birch tree watching the cottage.

Drained of anger and energy, she sat limply.
The stars came out like ice chips, chilling her, and
the tinfoil stream sang into its ferns.

You'll never be a gymnast, said a voice at the
edge of her mind.

"I hate you," she said to the Hooty Combe. "For
being so far away from Ferndale!"

She had never felt like that before! Shattered,
she clung to the birch tree. Every happy thing in
her life seemed suddenly to have gone — the sum-
mers, the squirrels in the wood, the primroses,
the snow. Gone, leaving nothing but gymnastics.
Even her parents whom she loved dearly now
stood like enemies between her and her ambitions.

Listening to her dad's footsteps coming home
up the lane, she felt worse and worse. Guiltily she
saw him open the cottage door and take Lynne in
his arms. She heard them talking. The birch tree
held her in cold white arms.

Bill stood in the garden.

"Anda!"

The Hooty Combe went quiet.

"Anda!"

She froze.

"I can see you. Act your age and come in. We've
got some talking to do!"

She would have to face the music! Slowly she
climbed down and walked back, heavily. Bella

trotted beside her anxiously, sensing the crisis.

Little was said, however, and the week drifted by. School and tea, and school, and breakfast. Guy Fawkes night passed in a blaze of sparks. Rain fell, and the Hooty Stream roared and frothed. Soon it was Monday again and, for the first time, Anda had neglected her training.

To her surprise, Bill took the afternoon off and both her parents drove to Ferndale with her after school. They parked Murgatroyd and came right into the gym!

Christie looked reproachfully at Anda. She raised her eyebrows questioningly.

"Problems last week?"

Anda looked back. For once she didn't smile. Christie was alarmed. Anda's sparkle had gone, and there was a sad little girl in its place!

"Mum and Dad are here. Dad says he wants to watch. Can he?"

But Christie had gone! "Great! I want to see them a minute!"

"Hi, Anda! Where've you been?" cried Julienne. "Have you been ill?"

Anda shrugged.

"Kerry even trained when she was ill. And she had an operation!" said Lena.

"I wasn't ill. Murgatroyd wouldn't start."

"Murgatroyd?"

"Our van."

"It's a heap," said Lena. "No wonder!"

"Shut up, Lena. You're a snob!" said Julienne sharply. She took Anda to one side, her blue eyes concerned. "Christie was cross. I tried to make excuses for you. You might have phoned — oh, you haven't got a phone, have you? I forgot. You should have been here last week. We went on the trampoline!"

"Did you get your award?" asked Anda.

"Yes. But John says I've still got to learn the vaults." A frown crossed Julienne's face. "Then we can both train with the squad!"

Anda shrugged. She looked so miserable that even Kerry spoke kindly to her.

"You'll be okay. We've all had problems, honestly," she said. "I should know!"

Anda looked at Kerry's small freckled face and saw courage there. For the first time she began to like Kerry.

The girls finished putting out the equipment, and started warm-up. John and Christie were outside the glass doors talking to Anda's parents! She could see them nodding and gesticulating and she would have given anything to listen!

At last they all came back into the gym. Bill and Lynne sat down on its floor. Anda ran over anxiously.

"We aren't here," announced Bill. "Take no notice of us. Go on. Get on with it!"

His eyes were twinkling.

"Come on, Anda." Christie whisked her away to work on the bars.

"You've got super parents!" she said. "They really do care and they are interested! We think we can work some transportation out for you, Anda. So if you work hard you can come on Thursdays and Saturdays, with my competition girls!"

"Oh! Oh, Christie!"

Anda's energy came back like a ball of fire. She felt she could jump as high as the ceiling!

"But they want to watch, just this once, to see what you're up to! Try to forget they're there — Okay?"

"Okay!"

"What are they doing here?" Julienne wanted to know as the two girls rubbed chalk on their hands. "My mum would like to watch and Christie won't let her!"

Hardly surprising, Anda thought. Julienne's mother was bossy and pushy. But she kept her thoughts to herself.

"I'm joining the competition girls!" she whispered. "If I work hard tonight! So we both can!"

"Oh super!" Julienne's friendly smile came on. Then a frown. "Honestly, it's not fair! I've been

51

coming here since I was six and I've only just made it! And you walk in and do it in six months!"

Anda shrugged. She felt awkward when Julienne got jealous.

Bars and beam were not part of the first four BAGA grades so their group concentrated on floor and vault for most of the lesson. Julienne's back flip was strong and sure.

But Anda made a mess of hers!

"Of course, you've had no practice for a fortnight, have you?" said Christie. "Have you been doing the exercises?"

Anda bit her lip. "Not properly. I was upset and I let it all go!"

"That's no excuse!" reproached Christie. "Well, come on, we'll work on it now!"

Again and again, with Christie supporting her, Anda flung herself backward onto her hands. It was no good! Yet two weeks ago she had done one, almost without support. She tried and tried. Then her limbs began to shake.

"All right, leave it," said Christie kindly. "Have a breather!"

But Anda shook her head. She didn't want to leave it. Especially with her parents sitting there!

"Why can't I do it?" she said, fighting the tears hard, and managing to stop them.

"I couldn't do it for ages, Anda!" said Julienne comfortingly. "Ages and ages!"

"You're not kidding!" joked Christie.

But Anda still felt frustrated because she couldn't do a back flip. She watched enviously as Julienne did hers.

Eventually Christie put her on the beam.

"Go on. Show your mum and dad what you can do!" she encouraged. "Go on. I want them to see!"

So up she went. She had progressed on the beam but she was allowed to do only what she'd been taught. Anda Barnes Specials were banned, Christie said! Dance steps, leaps and arabesques, a forward roll, and the splits she could manage. Tonight she was aware of Bill's intense blue eyes staring up at her as she worked. She resisted the temptation to show off!

But it was her vaulting that really made Bill's jaw drop.

"God!" he said quietly. "She's a human dynamo! I see what they mean about her. Do you, Lynne?"

"She frightens me!" said Lynne. "But I think it's marvelous. We mustn't stand in her way, Bill, if she's got that kind of talent."

6

The Competition Squad

Anda's first session with the Competition Squad was a shock. She arrived at the gymnasium with Julienne, her brain full of dreams.

"I'll bet we learn a new vault!" she said. "And we'll really be starting seriously on the beam and bars! I can't wait!"

For once Julienne was uncannily silent.

"Aren't you well?" asked Anda, thinking that Julienne's nose looked whiter than usual.

"No. I've got a stomachache."

Anda was about to sympathize when Lena's piercing voice interrupted.

"You've got nerves!" she shrieked. "Anyone can see that! Stomachache!"

"That's not true!" Julienne growled back. "Anyway, I wasn't even talking to you!"

"You wait! John and Christie are really hard on us this session."

54

"Oh, stop it, Lena," said Anda angrily, sensing Julienne's distress.

"She's as hard as nails," muttered Julienne as they followed Lena into the gym.

Lena turned.

"Hard as nails makes a good gymnast!" she said smugly. She ran to chat with the older girls.

"She'll get her comeuppance! Don't worry!" said Anda.

There were fourteen girls in the squad, six teenagers and eight younger girls, including Kerry, Anda, and Julienne.

Warm-up was much as usual, with a few harder exercises. The shock came afterward.

"Right, Julienne, Anda, Elizabeth, Spider Girl, Kerry, and Lena, go next door to ballet."

"Ballet!"

"Yes, ballet!" Christie grinned at Anda's shocked face. "We're lucky. We've got a proper ballet teacher on Thursdays."

Anda looked sadly at the mats and bars. All that tumbling time wasted! Doing ballet! Her body felt warm and bursting with energy. She ran up to Christie.

"Do I have to?"

"Yes, you have to. It's an essential part of your training. And so, I might add, is doing what you're told without question!"

Anda felt like arguing. Ballet! What a dirty trick!

But Christie had other people to think about besides Anda.

"Come on, Anda!" Julienne's eyes were sparkling. Stomachache gone! Ballet was what *she* had been looking forward to.

The dancing teacher was called Valerie. Anda thought she looked like a string puppet with elastic fingers and eyes like sour balls.

Fascinated and a bit resentful, she found herself a space.

"Let's see you stand first." Valerie had an unexpectedly earthy voice. She pounced on Anda straightaway.

"Look at you. With your bottom stuck out. Tuck it in. Pull your tummy in. Drop your shoulders."

She came and arranged Anda, patting her into place like a rag doll.

"Oh dear, you look crippled now. Drop your shoulders! What's your name?"

"Anda."

Walking was even worse.

"Pull your heads up! Tummy in, bottom in, toes pointed. No, not like that. For crying out loud! You can't even walk properly!"

Anda felt she must be the worst. She got angrier and angrier as she tried to cooperate.

"Pull your stomach in, Anda! You look like a banana walking along."

Anda stopped dead. A banana walking along, was she? She, Anda Barnes, who could do poetic cartwheels and fantastic back flips. Why should she be imprisoned with this Valerie and made to learn to walk?

"Move on, you're in everyone's way!"

But Anda stood, looking at the floor, a saucepan boiling inside her head.

"Oh, we're not going to sulk, are we?"

Julienne and Kerry were giggling. Unforgivable! But the sight of Julienne walking past like a majestic princess was comical. Giggling would destroy her silent protest, so she walked on after Julienne, with her mouth zipped tightly. Mercifully Valerie turned her attention to Lena. Apparently Lena was hopeless, too! She got called everything from a tin soldier to a daddy longlegs.

But Julienne didn't get "the treatment" at all.

"That's very good!" said Valerie. "You've got it. Walk round and we'll watch you!"

Begrudgingly, Anda thought Julienne did look elegant. She glanced at the clock. However much longer?

Next they learned some of the ballet positions, and then a step chassé.

57

Anda turned to Kerry.

"Don't we get to do any gymnastics this lesson?"

" 'Course we do. We've got another ten minutes with Valerie, that's all. Cheer up, Anda!" said Kerry kindly. "You'll like the next part. We have to do music and expression."

Valerie played some music, and asked them to dance to it, one by one.

"You can put in some cartwheels and things," she said. "If you want to. But nothing that needs support because I can't support you. The main thing is the music and the dancing. Listen to it and try to move with it. Who's going first?"

Anda shrank into the mat. She didn't want to dance with Valerie there criticizing her!

"I'll go!" said Julienne.

What she lacked in gymnastics, Julienne made up for in her dancing. She wasn't afraid to express herself. Anda was amazed at how good she looked.

"Well done!" said Valerie and Julienne rolled her eyes happily.

Anda went last, feeling bad inside. She considered the ballet positions and steps they had learned. Valerie's insults jarred in her brain and she felt inhibited. Her dancing by the Hooty Stream and on the beam for Christie was forgotten. She felt unable to move! The music started. She did two cartwheels and stood wondering what to do next.

"No, you mustn't stand and think!" cried Valerie. "Keep going! Oh, take your finger out of your mouth for goodness' sake, child!"

It was a nightmare. She moved, and stopped, and moved and stopped, and Valerie shouted at her, and the music escaped unnoticed across the ceiling. Her throat took over. She made for the door. The green and black corridor sped past and she was in the changing room, sobbing and sobbing, seeing people's shoes and bags gyrating through her tears.

No one rushed after her. She was alone, crying and ashamed of herself. How could she ever go back and face Valerie? Or Christie, after that?

Still sobbing she found her jeans and put them on, and pulled her sweater over her head. Hands in pockets she walked slowly out of Ferndale.

An astonishing sight met her eyes. Snow! Twisting and twinkling. The air like a great fridge. Snow, weeks before Christmas, icing everything.

Anda gazed in a surge of excitement. She wanted to rush and scoop it up in handfuls, to walk home, kicking it and feeling it on her face. Then she remembered it was her first time at Ferndale as part of the squad! If it hadn't been for that ballet lesson!

"Anda!"

Julienne was beside her.

"Where are you going? Wow! It's snowing!"

Together they watched the snow falling.

"Why have you got your jeans on?" asked Julienne.

Anda glowered. "That woman!"

"Who, Valerie?"

"Yes, *her*. If we're going to have *her* every week I'm not coming!"

"Oh, Anda! She isn't that bad! I like her."

"It's okay for you. You can do it."

Julienne bit her lip, hurt at her friend's anger.

"If you knew, Anda. The times I've been jealous of you. When you could do the vaults that I couldn't do. I mean, ballet's not difficult."

"It wasn't the ballet. It was *that woman*."

"Oh come on, Anda. We're in the gym now!" Julienne's blue eyes looked anxious. "Forget about it."

So she replaced her clothes and returned to the gym with Julienne, only to be stopped by a cold-eyed Christie.

"You aren't coming in here, madam," she said, "until you've apologized to Valerie."

"I'm not apologizing to *her*. *She* should apologize to me!" fired Anda, and the saucepan began bubbling again.

"If you are going to be a gymnast," said Christie coolly, "the first thing you will learn is discipline and respect for your coaches. Including Valerie."

"What do you mean?"

Anda stared at Christie, who had never before spoken to her so harshly.

"Exactly what I say. You go and apologize to Valerie. I don't care how hard it is or how much you hate it. And if you've got a discipline problem I don't want you in my squad."

Christie walked away. Anda opened her mouth to shout, "Who cares about your rotten squad," and shut it just in time to stop the words.

"I'll come with you," said Julienne kindly, but Christie called her away to practice walkovers. Anda hung at the door, torn between rushing out into the snow and being a child, or apologizing to Valerie and being a gymnast. What hurt the most was Christie's sudden coldness.

She shivered at the door, her legs and feet getting colder and colder. She would have to warm up all over again! What a waste of time.

"Hello, Anda. Got problems?"

Anda swung round and there was Valerie, her sour ball eyes looking straight into hers. The earthy voice sounded concerned, or was it mocking?

"No. I'm okay."

Valerie stood looking at her. "I'm sorry if I upset you," she said. "I've got a sharp tongue. You'll have to learn to laugh at me."

Anda couldn't believe her ears.

"But Christie said — I had to . . . " she choked, "apologize to you."

"Apologizing isn't being sorry. It's a mechanical act," said Valerie. "It's okay. Forget it. I expect I'm tougher than you!"

Her kindness was disarming.

"I am sorry, Valerie. Really."

"Forget it! We'll get along." Valerie patted her on the shoulder. "Go on. Go and do your flip-flans or whatever they are!"

"Flip-flans?"

"Flapjacks then!"

"Flic-flacs!" cried Anda and they both laughed.

She ran over to where Julienne was practicing round-off back flips.

"Have you? You have!" said Christie briefly to Anda. "We're practicing round off and two flips. Then we're going to learn a back somie on the trampoline, so get working!"

Anda made a dive for the mat and lunged into the tumbling sequence. But on the second back flip an excruciating pain in her leg made her cry out. She hopped away and sat down, catching her breath while the knot of pain tightened.

"What's the matter?" asked Julienne.

"I don't know."

"Your face has gone white! Christie! Anda's hurt herself!"

Christie came at once.

"It's not your day, is it?"

Anda shook her head, determined not to cry again! The pain eased. Christie made her lie face down.

"You've got cramp," she said. "At least I hope that's all it is. You're freezing cold, child! That's the worst thing for a gymnast. Put your track suit on and do some warm-ups. You know you shouldn't work cold! You could have pulled a muscle!" She called to one of the older girls, "Carol, do Anda's leg, will you?"

"I haven't got a track suit," said Anda, but Julienne was there straight away with hers.

"Put mine on. Go on, it doesn't matter!"

With Carol massaging her leg, and Julienne's track suit round her, Anda soon recovered. After some warm-ups she felt normal again. But she'd missed most of the floor work and Christie refused to let her vault.

"Not until you're sure that leg is okay. You work on the bar."

So she spent the last half hour working on the single bar, enjoying it, but feeling left out! Across the gym Julienne was having a good day! Sailing over the vault and getting praise from John.

The session finished with a lot of technical talk. The girls were given notebooks and told to write down everything they learned, and what exercises to do before Saturday. Then, to Anda's embarrassment, Christie said:

"Has anyone got an old track suit or some training tights they could lend or give to Anda?"

"I'll be getting one for Christmas," said Anda quickly. "And a leotard."

"Yes, but in the meantime," said Christie.

Surprisingly it was Lena who spoke up.

"I've got one you can have. It's only an old thing."

"Thanks," said Anda ungraciously. She didn't want to wear a track suit Lena had worn.

"By the way, you'll need competition leotards with the club badge eventually," Christie told them, pointing to a picture in a catalogue. "This is ours. This purple one."

"When can we enter something?" asked Lena.

"Well — there's the under-elevens County Championships next February. February 21st. You can enter if you want to, but don't expect to win anything. Just enter for experience and only expect a few marks each. We can enter a team or you can go as individuals," explained Christie.

Anda's eyes lit up. February 21st! Two months from now!

The snow was melting as they drove back to Elmsford.

"We get cut off if it gets really deep!" Anda told Julienne. "And I can't go to school!"

"You won't be able to get to gym club, either," said Julienne. "What if it snows on the 21st of February?"

"It won't," said Anda determinedly. "Or if it does, Dad will have to pull me there on a sled!"

"What's the 21st of February?" asked Julienne's mother.

"The under-elevens County Championships!"

"Oh darling! Your first competition! How wonderful!" gushed Julienne's mother. "We must get you entered at once! I must go up to town and get you a silk leotard and we'll do your hair up with a colored net pompon to match!"

Julienne didn't smile.

"Christie said we could enter if we want to, but not to expect high marks," explained Anda.

"I might not enter at all," said Julienne unexpectedly. She gave Anda a sharp nudge as if to warn her not to say anything.

Her mother's reaction was immediate. "Not enter! After all we've spent on your training! You most certainly will enter. And I shall be there to see you are fairly marked! Not enter indeed!"

7

You Will Not Fall

"Oh Julienne, you *can't* be worried about that vault. You can do squats with your eyes shut now!" said John. "If there's one thing I'm sure about for Saturday, it's you getting over the horse!"

Today was their last practice before the competition.

Julienne grinned and rolled her eyes.

"That's better!" said John. "You've got competition nerves. We all get them. Kerry's terrified!"

Kerry tried to look surprised. Her first competition since her illness was important to her.

"That's right, crack your freckles!" said John.

No one seemed to care about Kerry. Her parents weren't coming to watch her! She got herself to the club three times a week on an old bicycle, and nobody ever came with her or picked her up.

"Are you scared, Anda?"

"A bit," she admitted. "Mostly of the people watching!"

"Well, why do you do it, then, if you don't want anyone to watch?" teased John.

"I just love doing it," said Anda frankly.

John ruffled her hair.

"That's it, isn't it, Christie? That's the soul of the sport!" he said. "What are these? Paint-brushes?"

Anda giggled and pulled at the two ridiculously small bunches she had put her hair into. She longed to grow it into a bouncing ponytail like Lena.

In bed that night she mentally rehearsed her floor routine and thought of the group that was entering. She was worried for Julienne and Kerry. For herself she was confident of doing her best, and knowing that Bill and Lynne and Gran would love her whatever she did.

Under the wind and stars Hooty Cottage creaked cozily. Eventually Anda slept, excited, not dreaming that Saturday was to be the most dreadful day of her life!

When she arrived home from school on Friday, Lynne met her with a bright happy face.

"Go and look on your bed," she said.

"I'll just give Bella her tea," said Anda. "What can she have?"

"Treato!" said Lynne, producing a surprise tin of expensive cat food. Bella usually had scraps and goat's milk! Purring loudly she dug into the plateful Anda put down for her.

"Go and look upstairs! Go on!"

On her bed was an amazing sight. Lynne had washed her track suit and laid it out. Beside it was a neat white sports bag, a pair of brand new track shoes, thick white socks, and a purple competition leotard!

"Mum!" screamed Anda, throwing herself at Lynne who had followed her upstairs.

She couldn't believe her eyes. She'd expected to compete in her training leotard when everyone else had a purple one. "It doesn't matter," Christie had said. "As long as you're clean and tidy."

"But *Mum*. This is incredible! Where did it all come from? From Gran?"

"No. From us. I ordered the leotard from Christie's catalogue in time for the competition. Then we decided your shoes were a mess and you needed a neat bag, so I went shopping!"

Anda felt knocked out. She'd never before had new things except for birthdays or Christmas. She couldn't think where the money had come from!

"We didn't want to let the side down," explained Lynne. "You've practiced so hard, love, and Bill and I are so proud of you! We wanted you to have the best, and look as good as the other girls!"

"Oh, *Mum*." Anda fingered the new things wonderingly. "That's incredible. But. . . . "

"But what? Your eyes are out on stalks!" laughed Lynne.

"Well, I'm not going to win or anything!" said Anda anxiously, suddenly feeling she had to live up to the new clothes!

"No. We know that! But at least if you fall flat on your face you won't look scruffy."

"But I thought we were broke, Mum!"

Lynne sat down on the bed. "There is a 'but,' " she said slowly. "I was going to tell you first."

"What?"

"Well — it's the goats."

"The goats? Oh, what have they eaten now?" laughed Anda. "Not Christie's tumbling mat?"

"No, love. They've gone."

"Gone?"

"We've had to sell them. A man came and took them away this morning."

Millie and Mollie gone? Taken from home, in a truck with a strange man who might not love them!

"Well, say something!" said Lynne.

"I didn't want them to go." Anda stared at the floor. "They were born here. They'll feel — *lost*! Oh Mum! I didn't even say good-bye to them."

"Don't, Anda! They'll be okay. They've gone to

69

kind people. I didn't want them to go, either. Nor did Bill!"

Bill refused to be miserable.

"We can't sit moaning about them. They've gone and they'll survive. And we'll survive. We can't have it all ways. So let's be positive! Where's tea? Shall I heat up a can of soup?"

He bounded downstairs and started rummaging in the kitchen.

"He's wonderful," said Lynne. "He's upset and he's trying to be cheerful, and you've got to do the same."

So Millie and Mollie had been sold so that she, Anda Barnes, could look good! Suppose she did everything wrong after that! Suddenly the competition loomed with a different face.

Bill's cheerful example was difficult to follow. But she tried. She ate tea and chatted about everything but goats. A year ago she would have cried and raged. She was unaware how much gymnastics had changed her, and how grateful her parents were for the change!

Later she ran out to the cold barn for a last practice, passing the silent goat shed. She wore two sweaters, thick tights, and jeans. Hard as nails, she kept thinking. Hard as nails makes a good gymnast. Don't cry over Millie and Mollie.

Work till you hurt and the two goat faces will go away.

She worked at perfecting her agilities. The tinsica, the back walkover with change of leg, trying to get smooth, stretched, and flowing.

It wasn't until Bella came creeping under the door that she almost stopped for a cry over the goats. But Bella made her laugh. She whirled and climbed. She lay on her side and kicked the mat. She slid across the floor after chicken feathers.

After two hours she heard Bill's boots crunching down the path.

"Come on, Anda. It's eight o'clock. That's enough, surely?" he said. He stood watching her curl back to touch the floor and into a back walkover. "How can you *do* that?"

Anda was reluctant to stop.

"Have you looked outside?" said Bill. He took her arm and flung the door open. And there, in the yellow light from the barn, was a wild twisting snowstorm! A white crust clung to the door and drifts were forming triangles in the vegetables.

"A blizzard!" cried Anda.

In the swarming snow she danced and skated. Hundreds and thousands of snow dots sprayed her hot face and hands. The wind came in sneezes, almost knocking her over.

Bella was a hysterical snowball tearing in and out of the cabbages. Anda tried to scoop up enough snow for a ball to throw at her dad. Shaping its coldness in her hands she suddenly remembered the last time it had snowed.

"What if it snows on February 21st?" Julienne had said.

The snowball fell from her hand and smashed.

"Dad!" she began. "It's not going to last — is it?"

"Come on inside!" he urged, picking up Bella.

The living room was oven-hot. Anda tore off her sweaters and sat with her face pressed to the window.

"We've got to be there at ten in the morning," she said. "Gran's taking us, isn't she?"

"Yes."

"The snow will melt on the roads, won't it?"

Bill and Lynne looked at each other.

"Won't it, Dad?"

"Sometimes it does."

"They'll sand them, surely? Won't they?"

"If we're lucky."

"I wonder if Millie and Mollie are all right," said Anda, peering out at the speeding blizzard. "Do you think they've got a cozy shed? Do you think they'll be scared in a new place?"

Bill sighed.

"They had mountains of straw in the truck. And they've got each other," he said sadly. "It wasn't just your new clothes, you know, Anda. It was, well — taxes and Murgatroyd's battery and gas, and chicken food. Things like that."

"Anyway, you'd better get a good night's sleep, Anda," advised Lynne briskly. "You need to be fit tomorrow!"

"I think we all will!" agreed Bill. "How's your skiing?"

"I'll never sleep," said Anda. "Can I take Bella to bed? Please! Just tonight! I want her with me."

"Oh, let her," said Bill. "Take her box up. She won't stay in it, but never mind."

So with a last look at the snow, and a hot water bottle, cocoa, and Bella, Anda went up to bed.

"Will Gran be scared?" she asked Lynne. "Of driving in snow on slippery roads?"

"Probably. But Bill can drive. Try not to worry. See what the morning brings."

Bella sat demurely washing in her box. But as soon as Lynne had gone, she jumped on the bed. She walked round Anda's head, then lay on her chest, purring and staring with her green jewel eyes.

Anda got up and tried on her purple leotard. It fitted beautifully. She tried the hairband and admired herself in the mirror. The purple made her hair look golden. If only it would grow! She stared at her pink cheeks and brown eyes in the mirror, surprised that she looked quite pretty.

"You're going to do okay tomorrow, Anda Barnes," she told her face silently. "You will not fall off the beam. You will do your upstart on the bars properly. And you will not cry if it goes wrong!"

"Meow!" agreed Bella.

The purple leotard was hung up where she could see it. She leaned on the windowsill watching. Peaks of snow growing up the glass. Whirling whiteness out across the moor. A difficult journey tomorrow! An early start. But it never once occurred to her that she would not make it to the competition.

8
What if It Snows?

She awoke at six. Barely daylight but the room was full of strange white light from the snow. The wind had dropped and the sound of shoveling rang through the Hooty Combe.

Anda rolled out of bed. The day! The great day of the competition! She dressed at speed before peeping out of the window.

Snow curved and whipped like meringue. No grass. Only stalks and broccoli tops and bracken curls. The birch trees stood knee deep and the Hooty Stream was a tinkling chasm of black.

Anda gazed in silence. Half of it was magic, and half of it was terrible.

"You up already?" said Bill as Anda shot out of the back door.

"Dad! We aren't cut off. Are we? Are we?"

"I don't know until we try. Lots of villages are, according to the news."

"The main road will be okay. Surely?"

"Not at the moment it isn't. There's abandoned cars everywhere. They've got the snowplows out," said Bill.

"We are going, Dad. Aren't we? We've got to. I've got to be there. I've got to!"

"All right, cool it, Anda," he said. "We'll try. That's all I can promise. We might not even get out of Elmsford. I can't perform miracles."

"I've got to get there. I've got to," repeated Anda desperately.

"Well, you pray and I'll drive!" said Bill a bit angrily. "There's more snow on the way!"

"I hate the snow!"

Bill shook his head.

"Oh man! A kid of mine, hating the snow!" she heard him say as she went inside. Determinedly she packed her gymnastics clothes in the new white bag and slung it over her shoulder.

Lynne was in the kitchen behind a tower of sandwiches.

"Survival kit!" she said. "And you know I'm staying here in case you don't make it back tonight."

"Oh, Mum!"

"I'm disappointed. Terribly disappointed. But supposing we all three got marooned? What about Bella, and the chickens? They'd starve."

"I know."

Disappointment number one. Her mum not being able to come.

"Gran might not go, either. She's terrified of slippery roads," warned Lynne. She filled two thermos bottles, one with soup and one with coffee.

"You dress for the Arctic," she said. "Two sweaters. You might have to walk back here if you get stuck. I shall worry myself stupid!"

But for the competition, it would have been thrilling to set off on an expedition into the snow, fitted out for survival!

"We're crazy!" said Bill as they bumped out of the gate in Murgatroyd.

Seven o'clock. Surely three hours was long enough for them to get there, Anda thought.

It took ages to negotiate the lane. Where the snow was thin, Murgatroyd slid from bank to bank. Where it was thick, they had to dig.

"A good thing she's old and battered!" said Bill.

To start with it was fun. But the hand of Bill's watch moved steadily. Half past seven. Twenty to eight. Thank goodness for the downhill run to Gran's.

"Of *course* I'm coming!" Gran said indignantly when Bill explained how bad the roads were. "I started Anda off. I'm coming! You put the snow chains on the car and I'll be ready."

"Good old Gran!" said Anda, thinking how brave she was. "Mum said you were terrified."

"Nonsense. I've been miles in the snow." Gran unlocked the garage with a flourish. Bill dug away the surplus snow and started to fix the chains, one on each wheel. Precious minutes were ticking away.

Gran reappeared dressed in a sheepskin coat, trousers, and thick boots. They finally left at half past eight.

"We'll never get up the hill. I'll try the toll road," said Bill. "And let's hope the main road will be cleared by now."

The toll road was a long detour round the foot of the moors. With Bill driving, Gran's car clicked along bravely like a little boat sailing out.

Nine o'clock and the white road wound ahead completely deserted.

"If we keep this speed up, you might just make it for warm-up, Anda," Bill said optimistically. "What time's the actual competition start?"

"Eleven," said Anda, and her stomach started to rumble with nerves and hunger.

Wine-dark clouds loomed ahead. The wind rose, whipping dry snow off the hedges and across the road. Suddenly the air was full of ice-cream sprinkles again.

"That's done it," sighed Bill. "Another blizzard. Now we are in trouble."

"Keep going!" said Gran. "At least make it to the main road."

"Quite honestly it would be better to turn back. Look, the windshield wipers are hardly coping. It's madness to go on!"

"Oh no, Dad!" cried Anda.

"Go on," said Gran. "We've got a chance."

"You'll wish you'd listened to me!" said Bill anxiously.

Reluctantly he kept driving and Anda sat back in relief. She started worrying about missing warm-up and the shame of being late.

The blizzard got thicker and Bill got angrier.

"Don't stop!" pleaded Gran. "Or we'll get stuck."

"I can't go any faster. It's deeper here. There's a dip in the road."

The car rolled into a patch of deep snow and stopped with its engine roaring.

"That's it!" said Bill grimly. He tried to reverse out of it but the car wouldn't move.

"Come on, Anda. We'll push," said Gran gamely.

They got out, into the blizzard.

"Push her back!" shouted Bill. "Not forward!"

While the wind was whisking snow along the ground, piling it against the wheels, they pushed against the hood. Gran wheezed and Anda giggled. She knew she shouldn't be giggling but it struck her as hilariously funny, pushing a car that wouldn't move.

At last Bill took the shovel from the trunk.

"I'll have to dig her out. It's getting deeper by the minute."

He took one look at Gran's purple-red face through the whirling snow and said, "You get back in. Go on. You'll make yourself ill."

But Gran wouldn't. She stood in the snow, wheezing, trying to scrape it away with her boots.

"Here you are, toughie. You shovel, too." Bill handed Anda the coal shovel. She started to dig furiously, getting hotter and hotter with the snow streaming past her face. Beside her Bill dug like a madman, blowing and swearing. The faster they worked, the more the wind flung snow over the car. Soon the windows and doors were plastered.

Bill had another go at revving the car. The engine whined and strained, but the wheels stayed locked. He got out again and threw his shovel as far as he could throw it. Anda was startled. Bill rarely lost his temper but he had now.

"Will you GET IN the car!" he hollered at Gran who was gasping for breath.

"I won't be spoken to like that!" she wheezed.

Bill took her arm and wrenched the car door open.

"You are to get in or you'll BE ILL," he shouted.

"And then we'll need an ambulance. Now get in and stay in and do as you are told, woman!"

Gran got in, looking upset, and shut the door.

"You can rev her if you like, and we'll dig. If I can just get her turned round we can go back."

"But Dad. What about . . . " began Anda, her dreams of the competition toppling.

"Don't you whine!" he snapped. "We've done our best to get you there and we can't. So that's it. Just don't grizzle!"

He fetched his shovel. Snow was driving thickly over the road, covering their wheel tracks.

"Oh please, Dad. Can't we. . . . " she tried to say as his red face and snow-blotted beard loomed up in the snow.

He put a snowy arm round her.

"I'm sorry I got mad," he sighed defeatedly. "Look — just try and be brave, Anda. I'm sorry about the competition. Just for goodness' sake don't cry."

Anda took a deep breath and pulled her shaking knees together.

"I wasn't," she said. "Come on, let's try digging again."

But with the car completely stuck, and the blizzard worsening, it was hopeless.

"Take your parka off and shake it. We'll get in and decide what to do," said Bill wearily.

Inside, the car was a warm cocoon.

"Are you okay?" Bill asked Gran.

"Yes, I'm fine." Gran had recovered enough to sip coffee. "What's the best thing to do? You're the survival expert!"

Bill considered.

"There's no sign of it stopping," he said. "You realize the car could get completely buried?"

Gran nodded. "I know."

"We could stick with it. Or walk back to Elmsford, about five miles. I doubt if we'll get any help. There'll be too many people stuck!"

Anda sat in the back, silent, her thoughts in a corked-up bottle. Bill had said, "Don't grizzle," and so she didn't. She avoided looking at the white bag or at Bill's watch.

Soup and a sandwich were handed over to her.

"Eat it quickly. The sooner we go the better," said Bill.

They had decided Gran should stay in the car and keep warm, while Bill walked back into Elmsford for help.

"I should think you're fit enough to come with me, Anda, aren't you? Then Gran can have all the blankets and the food. She's got to keep warm."

Anda swallowed her soup and stuffed the sandwich down.

Reluctantly they left Gran, bundled up in blankets, alone in the car. She waved and smiled cheerfully.

"Come on, kid," said Bill. "Stick right behind me and walk in my tracks. We'll make it."

Anda had no words left. Numb-throated, she followed Bill's dark green raincoat and tall boots along the silver white road.

On and on they walked in a strange rhythm, their backs to the wind. Images came into Anda's mind. Julienne dancing. Lena on the beam. Kerry's determined freckles. The high leather vaulting horse. Herself in the purple leotard. The audience clapping. The hours and hours of practice when nobody clapped. Black boots and soaking jeans walking, walking through the powdery snow.

Bill turned to see if she was okay.

Her small face with its big shiny eyes looked up at him from the hood of her parka and a halo of dripping wet hair.

"You all right?"

She shrugged inside her heavy clothes.

"Yep."

"Don't be too sore over the competition. There'll be others. Christie will understand," he said, taking her hand.

Anda shrugged again. Two tears rolled down her face, but she didn't sob.

"There are other priorities right now," said Bill.

"You realize Gran is in danger! Old people can be very ill from exposure. Or even die!"

"No. I didn't know!"

"She'll be okay for a few hours. But we must get someone out to her! That's why I'm walking as fast as I can. Are you keeping up all right?"

"Yes," said Anda, and added cheekily, "I'm fitter than you any day! Poor Gran! She didn't want to come really."

They walked on and Anda sank back into her gloom.

"There is a future after today, you know!" said Bill. "You can still train with the squad. You've still got your talent, Anda. There'll be lots of competitions for you."

He scrubbed the snow from a signpost.

"Elmsford one mile!" he cried. "We're nearly there!"

One o'clock and they were trudging through the new development like two snowmen. Gran's yellow front door had never looked so friendly to Anda. People could die in blizzards! Hours of wading through snowdrifts and her worries about the competition had faded. Staying alive was important now. Forcing her legs to keep walking, carrying the lead weight of wet clothes. Worrying about Gran left alone, perhaps scared, perhaps dying from cold.

Bill went straight to the phone.

"You get in the bath," he ordered Anda. "Go on."

He rang the police and told them where Gran was.

Anda stood in the bathroom looking at herself in the mirror. February 21st! Instead of dancing in a purple leotard, there she stood in a dripping brown parka with hair like wet spaghetti. What a waste of a gymnast!

She lay in a steaming blue bath. Then she padded into Gran's bedroom and borrowed a big woolly jacket to wrap herself in. Was Gran dead? Gran, who had given her the chance to do gymnastics. And what about her mum, alone at Hooty Cottage in the blizzard? And Bella?

But Gran was very much alive! She was rescued by two policemen and carried through the snow to their Landrover. An hour later she arrived home in it, eyes sparkling with excitement. She refused to sit down but bustled round getting tea and putting wet clothes in the drier.

"For you two heroes," she said. "You both deserve a gold medal for walking all that way in the snow. Especially Anda! It must have been up to your waist!"

Anda smiled. It was good to feel brave. Afterward! And Gran had thoughtfully remembered to bring Anda's precious white bag with her in the Landrover.

"I'm really disappointed at not seeing you compete today," she said warmly. "Perhaps I can come to the club and watch you?"

"If Christie ever lets me in the door again!" said Anda.

"I'll ring her up," said Gran spiritedly. "And tell her what we've been through trying to get there!"

And she did. Later that evening when they had decided to stay the night with Gran rather than attempt to walk to Hooty Cottage in the dark.

"There you are. You talk to her!"

She waved the phone at Anda.

"No," mouthed Anda, thinking Christie would be angry.

Gran forced the phone into her hand.

"It's okay, Anda. I know you couldn't help it. You must have been shattered!" said Christie's voice kindly.

"I was," said Anda. "We tried. We left at seven o'clock."

"Lots of people didn't make it. Kerry didn't. Julienne was late — and she made a mess of it — oh dear!" went on Christie. "What a day! Lena fell flat on her face on the bar and got a nosebleed. She is human by the way!" she joked.

"Oh!" So other people had had a bad day, too!

"Anyway, so few kids turned up because of the snow that they've decided to hold it again — in April probably — so you'll still be able to enter!"

"Oh, great!" said Anda.

"And there's another one in March — a floor and vault competition at Ferndale," said Christie. "And there's a training weekend, and a trip to London, all sorts of things, so cheer up."

On Sunday morning she was at last able to enjoy the magic of the snow. Through diamond drifts she and Bill climbed the lane to Hooty Cottage. The cottage looked like a peppermint palace. Lynne stood at the door with Bella in her arms, relieved to see them.

Anda spent the morning skidding and rolling in the snow and cracking the ice around the Hooty Stream. She sat in the birch tree, sucking an icicle, thinking ahead to the floor and vault competition in March. This time nothing must go wrong! Nothing, nothing must go wrong!

9

Please Let Me Enter

The train from the West Country pulled in at Paddington Station. The group of gymnasts from Ferndale jumped out, talking and laughing.

"Now we get the Underground to Wembley," said Christie.

Anda was completely bewildered. She hadn't been to London before.

Julienne was scornful. "I've been here heaps of times!" she yawned. "This is nothing, Anda. You should see the big shops. Mummy brings me every year Christmas shopping, and we get squashed to death. It's awful. Come *on!*"

Anda had stopped again to talk to the pigeons. She was sorry for them.

"Christie's *gone!*" cried Julienne, almost pulling her over. Giggling, they tore across Paddington Station, around people and over suitcases.

Next she was frightened to step on the escalator

until Christie said, "What, you! A gymnast! Frightened to step on that!"

Anda stepped on at once, her face red.

Downstairs she was even more terrified of the underground train taking her into a tunnel that roared and puffed like a dragon's nostril. She clung to Julienne, giggling to hide her nervousness, until they came out into the street at Wembley.

"She hasn't said a word since we got here!" laughed Julienne, intrigued to see Anda actually scared of something.

"You'll have to get used to traveling if you're going to be a gymnast!" John said. "What about International Competitions, Anda? We can't pack you in a parcel and have you delivered! One country mouse. If lost, please return to sender."

Anda grinned.

Once inside Wembley Arena, it was worth it. They had come to watch the finals of a national gymnastics competition.

The competition began with *March of the Champions*. While the audience clapped in time, in marched the teams and the arena was full of color. Tiny gymnasts, each team in matching leotards, strutted in proudly with high chins and pointed toes. Watching them Anda realized why Valerie had fussed about her learning to walk!

"Why isn't there anyone from Ferndale?" asked Anda.

"Oh we tried!" said Christie. "We always enter!"

"Perhaps it'll be you down there one day!" said John, leaning round to speak to Anda.

"I wish it was!" she answered.

How lovely to march around with everyone clapping, she thought. But when the actual competition started, she couldn't imagine how long it would take her to reach that standard!

"Can I enter next year?" she asked Christie.

"No, love," Christie smiled gently. "You aren't old enough or experienced enough."

"If I train extra, extra hard?"

"No. You can't push it, Anda! Superman wasn't built in a day. He took years!"

"I wish I could wake up in the morning and find I could do everything!" said Anda sadly.

"There'll be plenty of little local things you can enter. Cheer up!" said Christie kindly. "You walk before you can run!"

Anda sighed. She opened a bag of potato chips and shared them with Julienne, munching and thinking as she watched the polished performances. Briefly she thought of Hooty Cottage and her parents. Her training was making things difficult for them. Lynne missed the goats, and Bill was doing long hours bricklaying instead of the gardening he loved. She felt guilty, but she couldn't give it up. What really worried her was something Bill had said about Murgatroyd. Murgatroyd only had another week before her yearly inspection. She would fail, and there was no money to put her right. And without Murgatroyd she could not get to Ferndale on Saturdays!

But during the lunch break at Wembley, Anda made a fantastic discovery.

She and Julienne were browsing round the stands in the foyer. Julienne had bought herself a BAGA T-shirt and some badges. Anda had brought half her piggy bank to spend. She bought a can of soda pop, which she wasn't allowed at home.

Suddenly a poster caught her eye. A young gymnast, and the words SOUTH WEST TRAINING AWARD in large letters, and PLEASE TAKE A LEAFLET.

She took one of the glossy folders and opened it.

What she read filled her with excitement.

"I've *got* to find Christie!" she said. "I've *got* to enter this. I've *got* to!"

She was jumping up and down.

"Have you gone nuts?" asked Julienne.

"No. Look!"

"Oh that. Yes, I saw it. Good, isn't it?"

Julienne was still busy choosing badges. She already had a large collection sewn on her parka. Anda searched for Christie. She and John were in the arena, talking to a man in a black track suit.

Too shy to walk across there, Anda waited impatiently at the steps, knowing she would get snubbed for interrupting. At last they came toward her.

"Christie!"

Anda thrust the leaflet into Christie's hand.

"Can I enter this? I've got to, Christie. Please let me. Please. It's specially for people like me!"

"Hang on a minute. Cool it!"

"It's a training award! Two hundred pounds a year to cover things like clothes and transportation and training weekends," said Anda, her eyes sparkling. "And it's for under-twelves!"

Christie flicked through the leaflet.

"What a super idea!" she said. "This is something new!"

"But can I?"

"It looks hopeful," sighed Christie. "But I did *tell* you, Anda, you may not be able to *this* year. You just haven't got the experience."

"But it does say even beginners can enter!"

"I know. I know. But you don't realize what you'd be up against, Anda! The competition will be hot for this, I can tell you!"

"But I could *try*. Then Mum and Dad could have the goats back!"

"I'll discuss it with John," was all Christie would say.

Intensely disappointed, Anda returned to her seat. She read the leaflet through about six times. Christie hadn't said no. And she hadn't said yes.

The day passed in a blur of medal ceremonies and train journeys. The training award suddenly became *thought number one* in Anda's head. She tried asking John, but he only said:

"We'll see. You haven't even entered a competition yet, Anda. *You* don't know how you're going to react. You might be a bag of nerves!"

"I won't be," she said stubbornly.

"Well — see how you do next week. Then we'll decide. I'll discuss it with Christie," said John. "Don't get too intense over it. What's the big hurry? You're only ten!"

"It's not that I want to win medals or anything," sighed Anda. "It's Mum and Dad. They wanted to be self-sufficient and now they can't because of me."

"All parents make sacrifices for their kids," said John. "Some parents have even moved house for their kids to be near the gym club!"

The idea of leaving Hooty Cottage tore at Anda's thoughts. It only made her more determined to enter for the training award. See how you do next week? Right, she'd show them! she thought. Next Sunday was the floor and vault competition at Ferndale.

10

The Day of the Purple Leotard

Sunday dawned clear and crisp. Anda was awake early, dreading to see snow again. March lambs cried up on the moor and the Hooty Combe glittered with primroses. Bella was leaping and twisting after a butterfly. Anda watched her thoughtfully, thinking how she loved the little cat. It was almost a year since she had rescued her from the church roof — a year of gymnastics!

"Make the most of it, Anda!" said Bill as they set off. "This is Murgatroyd's last trip, probably."

"Is it her test tomorrow?"

"Yes. She won't pass. She needs a lot of expensive work. She'll have to go to the great garage in the sky."

"What's going to happen, Dad? Are we going to get a new one?"

Bill hit the ceiling. "A new one! Of *course* not. You can't just *get* another car. Just click! Like that."

"But — what will we do for transportation?" asked Anda, anxious about getting to Ferndale on Saturdays, and to competitions and weekend events Christie had planned.

"Wait and see. I might manage a moped," said Bill. "You could ride on the back."

"I'd love that!" cried Anda, imagining herself arriving at Ferndale like a Hell's Angel.

"You might not," said Lynne. "Or Bill might get a salesman's job with a flash car to go with it."

Bill gripped Murgatroyd's wheel tighter.

"Just lay off, will you, Lynne," he snapped.

"I was only. . . . "

"Well you *know* how I feel about it. There's no need to start this in front of Anda."

He changed gear with a roar. Lynne sulked.

Anda's first competition. The day of the purple leotard! And her parents were miserable!

"If I do okay today, Christie's going to let me enter for this training award, Dad."

"Great. You have to try. But don't feel you've got to."

"Fat chance!" growled Lynne. "We've never been awarded anything!"

In upset silence they traveled the rest of the way. Anda remembered hearing her parents up late arguing. About money, she imagined. Money, and transportation, and having a child who was a gymnastics addict. Winning the training award would change that. So today was vital. Decision day. She was glad to see Gran's cheerful face when they reached Ferndale.

"I'll do her hair, dear. You sit down. You look awful!" she said. She hurried Anda into the changing room.

"What's it going to be? Two little pigtails?" she asked.

"Yes."

Anda's hair had grown but not enough for the coveted single ponytail. Gran had made her two purple pompons on elastic to match the leotard.

"There, you do look sweet!" she crowed, dapping round with the comb.

"Aw!" jeered Kerry mischievously.

Anda gave her a passing smack.

The changing room was full of gymnasts and fussing parents. Sixty children under eleven from clubs all over the county. Anda glanced at odd individuals, wondering how good they were. A cool, hard, experienced lot, she thought jealously. How she wished she had started younger. Seeing children smaller, calmer, and apparently tougher than her was frightening. But she soon found out that others were as nervous as she was.

Julienne arrived looking white-faced.

"I don't need any help, Mummy. Really I don't!" she was saying. "My hair's okay like this."

She had her braids in two loops, one each side, and a purple leotard like Anda's to show she belonged to Ferndale.

"Hi, Anda! You look *wow*!" she cried. "Are you going in for warm-up now? Wait for me. Please wait. I'll be quick. I don't need you, Mummy, really I don't."

"Oh, but you — "

"*Please*, Mummy. Leave me. Please!"

Gran took in the situation. She bustled Julienne's mother away like a long-lost friend.

There were four entries from Ferndale. Anda, Julienne, Lena, and Kerry. No one was with Kerry. She looked good, but was strangely quiet. She stayed close to Anda and Julienne.

Anda glanced briefly at the chattering audience sitting on chairs around the twelve-meter floor area. During warm-up Anda was aware of Bill's blue eyes watching her. And Gran's surprised face. They couldn't take their eyes off her. They were proud of her. It felt good.

Warm-up was difficult, with such a crowd. Colored bodies flew past Anda doing flic-flacs and dive rolls, their coaches crab-walking beside them. Some of them looked fantastically good! She couldn't find a space to practice her own tumbling run, until Christie came to help her. She got a lecture as well.

"You watch your concentration, young lady! Your eyes are all over the hall. Never mind who is doing what! You concentrate on *you*. Okay?"

"Okay."

"And don't forget to present yourselves to the chief judge!" said Christie. "She's there. In that corner!"

Anda looked at the chief judge, who was just settling into her chair. She didn't look frightening.

The floor was cleared and the gymnasts lined up in the corridor outside, ready for march-in.

"I've been looking forward to this part," whispered Anda.

"So have I," Julienne whispered back.

"Silence!" bellowed John.

They stood like soldiers, waiting. The Ferndale group was third in the line with six gymnasts ahead of them, two in yellow and four in royal blue. Then came Lena, Julienne, Kerry, and Anda, and a long line of gymnasts behind them.

The music started. A bolt of excitement ran through Anda. Then it was happening. She was marching in, head high, toes pointed, carefully leaving the right space between her and Kerry, and not looking to the right or left.

"You've got to be absolutely poker-faced," Christie had said.

The audience rose to the occasion and clapped in time. And they applauded every group as it was presented. Anda was the smallest in her group. She stretched and waved. Straight ahead of her she glimpsed her parents and Gran, their hands going like drumsticks, and that made her smile.

The competitors were split into two groups. Group B marched out to do their vault, which was set up in the hall. Group A, Anda's group, sat on benches to wait. Behind the benches were some mats for last minute warm-ups before their turn.

The girls who started weren't particularly good! Certainly not up to Lena's standard. But probably better than her, Anda thought. None of them danced as well as Julienne!

Lena began to warm up behind her. Suddenly Anda was aware of Kerry sitting next to her. Kerry's whole body was trembling and she had pressed her hands over her temples.

"What's the matter?" Anda asked gently.

Kerry shook her head.

"I can't," she whispered. "I can't go on."

"Why?"

"Look at me! I want to and I can't. I don't know how to stop it."

Kerry shook even more violently. Julienne, who was getting keyed up for her own performance, put her arm round her.

"Don't, Kerry. You'll be okay!"

"Warm up," advised Anda. "Christie said to, if we got really nervous."

"I feel really sick and giddy!" whispered Kerry. She dropped her face into her hands. Anda looked round for Christie. But Christie was operating the tape recorder.

"I'll withdraw," said Kerry. "Tell Christie."

"You can't, Kerry. It's only nerves! Go on, warm up!"

But Kerry wouldn't move. Julienne and Anda looked at each other helplessly. Suppose Kerry really was ill?

Lena was walking out. Only two more! Then Anda! Her heart began to thrum and her hands were sweating.

"You're making me nervous!" she whispered to Kerry. "Look — Lena's going!"

White-faced, Julienne warmed up. An inner calm kept her together, even though she was as nervous as Kerry.

Kerry sat up, gripping the bench with both hands. She took deep breaths, watching Lena.

Lena's performance was fast, snappy, and efficient. Anda watched enviously. If she could tumble like Lena and dance like Julienne! But she had hardly time to think about herself. Next to her Kerry had forced herself to action, her freckled face damp and tight. Anda took her own suit off. She did some stretches and walkovers, half-watching Julienne's poetic routine.

Julienne got a huge clap, and a cheer that sounded like Bill's! She walked back, rolling her eyes, her face pink. And Kerry was going out, presenting herself to the judge, waiting for her music.

Kerry was elfin-thin. She could do aerial cartwheels and high-tucked somersaults. She danced with cobweb fingers and a deep frown.

"Don't frown, Kerry!" Christie had said many times, but Kerry always did.

Completing her routine in front of an audience was a devastating achievement. She walked back with a magical smile, almost giggling with delight. The audience clapped, but there was no one special to cheer her.

Now Anda's turn.

A rush of nerves, sudden determination. An explosive strength within her that must be perfectly controlled, perfectly guided into a perfect performance.

A haze of faces. A long moment as she waited like an unlit firework for the judge to nod at her.

"Absolute concentration," Christie had said.

"Perform in your own little world. Concentrate all your energy within yourself and don't waste a drop!"

The judge nodded, pencil ready, glasses flashing.

Anda presented herself as elegantly as she could and walked to her starting point.

Her music had a bubbling rhythm with sudden stops and runs. She danced and ran into her first tumbling sequence, a round off, two flic-flacs, and a back straddle roll, putting speed and stretch into it.

Across the room Christie held her breath and sweated. Little Anda had put more amplitude into her opening sequence than Christie had expected. She was terrified Anda would get over-enthusiastic and crash or make a wild attempt at an agility that was not in her routine. But she didn't.

Synchronizing her ballet steps and arm movements with the music as Valerie had taught her, Anda curved and twisted, working in a tinsica, walkovers, handsprings, cartwheels. She knew the routine like clockwork, and she tried to give it extra grace and polish. Her dive roll was the highest she had ever done, her final pose well-timed. The precious minute had passed! She walked off, trying to look dignified, hearing Bill whistling and cheering and everyone clapping.

Had she done okay? She thought she had. No mistakes, only a slight twist in landing from her handspring. And she had tried desperately hard. Bill looked across at her and pounded the air with his fist. He had a massive smile. Even Lynne looked happy now! But best of all were Christie's raised eyebrows and nod of approval.

"That was good, Anda!" said Lena, to her surprise.

"You were *wow!*" said Julienne.

"So were you!"

"Shh!"

They were supposed to be quiet. It was difficult after they had performed. Anda glanced at Kerry.

"Are you okay now?" she mouthed.

Kerry nodded and beamed.

John came up behind them and put his arms round them both. Kerry started to chatter.

"Shh!"

Anxiously they waited for the marks, which were read out in groups. Christie had told Anda and Julienne not to expect more than four or five.

Lena had eight-point-six, the highest mark so far in the competition. Then Julienne's mark.

"Julienne Wellington. Five-point-eight."

John gave Julienne a pat, but she looked gloomy. Anda knew it was because of her mother. "I'll get three," she was thinking. "I couldn't be as good as Julienne."

"Kerry Bartlett, seven-point-nine-five."

Better than Kerry had expected. Her face broke into a smile.

"Anda Barnes, seven-point-two."

"What!"

That couldn't be right! She couldn't have scored all that! More than Julienne? Almost as much as Lena!

Bill let out a cheer. Anda was embarrassed. She could see Gran trying to shut him up. She ought to have told him that spectators had to behave!

She turned to John in amazement.

"They've made a *mistake*!" she whispered.

"Why?"

"I can't have scored all that. You said — "

"No. That's about right," he murmured. "Boy, did you rise to the occasion! Paintbrush!"

He gave one of her little pigtails a tug and walked off. He only called her "Paintbrush" when he was pleased with her! She sat in a daze. Happiness spread over her like sunshine.

After lunch Anda's group warmed up for the vault. Two tries each were allowed. Anda had badly wanted to do a handspring vault, which she was quite good at, but John had said, "No — not

105

in your first competition!" so she was doing a straddle, which carried a lower tariff.

This time Julienne was upset. Vaulting was not one of her strengths, and she knew it. She fell awkwardly, then chickened and missed her turn.

"I'll never get over. It's the timing. My run up goes all wrong," she said to Anda. "John's cross with me. I know he is. He thinks it's psychological." Julienne was rubbing her ankle. "I think I twisted it when I fell."

"You ought to tell Christie!"

"It might be all right. I'll leave it."

"Christie's talking to your mum," said Anda. "And Valerie is."

"Oh no. They're arguing!" sighed Julienne. "I hope Mum isn't complaining about my marks."

Certainly Julienne's mother looked ruffled, and so did Christie. But to everyone's surprise. Julienne managed a neat squat vault and scored three for it.

Soon it was Anda's turn. She took a deep breath and fixed the leather horse in her eye. Straight ahead. Speed. Power. Don't look at Gran! She was over, and walking back for her second vault.

John was standing by the horse.

"Straight legs," he had said as she finished.

So she tried, but pitched forward on landing.

She scored five. Not bad for a low tariff vault.

Now they were free to sit with their parents until the final march-in and medal presentation.

"You were terrific!" said Bill, giving Anda a cuddle.

"I don't know how anyone your size can get over that great thing!" said Gran, waving a hand at the vaulting horse.

"I shut my eyes!" said Lynne.

"Mummy, you didn't!"

"I did!"

"But you never saw me vault!"

"No, but I opened my eyes in time to see you were still alive and not scattered all over the hall!"

Anda giggled. Her parents looked more cheerful now.

"I've chatted to Christie," Bill told her. "She's going to put you in for this South West Training Award thing — but she did say you only had the slimmest of chances. You aren't really experienced enough."

"Oh, great!" Anda's eyes sparkled.

"You did better than she expected today!"

"I know. I've just been lucky! It's been a perfect, perfect day for me!" smiled Anda. She wouldn't get a medal, but her marks and Christie's promise were enough to make her high. She felt like singing and dancing.

"We ought to celebrate!" said Bill. "Why don't we?"

"What with?" asked Lynne.

Bill dug in his jeans pocket and produced some change.

"A bottle of cheapo wine for us and soda pop for Anda."

"And Bella can have some cream!" said Anda.

At the end of the day, Lena had come in second in the overall marking, and Kerry was third in the vaulting.

"We aren't too far down the list!" said Anda as she and Julienne stood looking at the marks after the final march-in. Everyone was going home and the sound of chairs being stacked rang around the hall. Kerry cycled off by herself with her precious medal in her hand on a joyfully zig-zagging bike.

"Our first competition!" sighed Anda. "Wasn't it terrific! I wish we could do it all over again!"

"Your first. And my last, probably."

"Julienne! What do you mean?"

Julienne had been oddly quiet ever since the vaulting. Now she dropped her bombshell.

"I might give it up."

"Give it up! What, give up gymnastics? You can't! You must be crazy!"

Julienne silently stared at her toe drawing patterns on the floor. Her blue eyes had black clouds in them.

"Why?" persisted Anda, but her friend couldn't seem to answer. "Does Christie know?"

"Yes," said Julienne slowly. A tear rolled down her cheek.

"But why? Oh don't, Julienne!"

Suddenly Julienne was sobbing violently, her head against the wall.

"I can't — can't stop!" she choked, and shook Anda's hand away. "Leave me, just leave me."

"But — "

"LEAVE ME!"

Anda stood, alarmed, wanting to help. Together they'd survived some tough training sessions. She had seen Julienne hurt and afraid, insulted by Lena, shouted at by John, but never had she seen her cry.

Lynne came up.

"Whatever is wrong with Julienne?"

But Julienne went on sniffing and gulping against the wall.

"Where's your mother?"

"She's in — in — in — the car." The words came in jumps. "She's wait— waiting for me. I don't want her."

"You can tell us, love!"

Julienne leaned against Lynne. Eventually the story came out, in bursts and sobs.

"Christie thinks I haven't — haven't. . . . "

"All right, take your time!" crooned Lynne, stroking Julienne's hair.

"Christie said I haven't got the nerve for gymnastics."

"Oh you have!" cried Anda, wanting to comfort her friend, but even, as she said it, she knew Christie was right.

"No. It's true. It's — it's okay for people like you and Lena," wept Julienne. "You don't get scared — not scared of vaulting or bar work. I do. I'm scared all the time and Christie knows. There's no way I can hide it anymore."

"Then it's best to give up, surely? After all you *are* a brilliant dancer!" said Lynne gently.

"It's my mum, really," went on Julienne in a torrent of words and tears. "She wanted me to be brilliant and I'm not. She pushed Christie into training me really and she's given a lot of money to the club and so Christie sort of had to, I suppose. It was okay while we were just doing our BAGA awards, but now it's got too difficult — Christie said I'd reached my limits and I couldn't get any better. She said did Mummy want me to be badly injured to prove the point, and that shut her up. She's been talking to Valerie about ballet."

"Oh, poor Julienne!" said Anda. "You're my best friend, Julienne, honestly. I don't know what I'll do at the club without you!"

Gradually Julienne was unwinding.

"I'll still come on Mondays. Christie said just to come and enjoy myself and I'd be welcome! She said perhaps I could help her start the little ones off."

"Well, you'd like that, wouldn't you?" asked Lynne.

"I suppose. I do like little kids."

"Perhaps you could be a coach when you get older!" suggested Gran. They were all standing there now, round poor Julienne.

"You can still come to tea and jump the Hooty Stream!" said Bill. "And I want free tickets for your *Swan Lake*, okay?"

That produced a watery smile. Before long they had calmed Julienne down between them.

"Can't you come back with us to tea?" she asked. "Ask your mum."

"Okay."

They walked to the car with Julienne. Her mother was waiting, drumming her fingers on the steering wheel.

"Well, no," she said when Lynne asked her about tea. Her usual bossy manner had softened. "I've been sitting here thinking. I was going to take

Julienne out or something. She's had a hard time. I've been too . . . well — it's difficult."

Lynne nodded. "Okay. Perhaps another day?"

"Of course. And we'll still take Anda on Mondays — don't worry."

The two women smiled at each other.

"Perhaps she has got a heart after all," said Lynne as Mrs. Wellington drove off with Julienne, solemn-faced, in the front seat.

"She needs a kick in the — "

"Bill!" said Gran sharply.

"Well! She does. I wouldn't want *my* kid going through that!" His blue eyes were angry.

"I don't. I love it!" said Anda anxiously.

"I know. There's no way Christie's going to throw you out!" said Bill. "But promise me, Anda, you won't get in a mess like that! If ever you get too scared, or bored, you are to stop. I don't care if you never win anything. Just be happy. The training award doesn't matter!"

"It does!" said Anda. "And I am happy, Dad!"

Not even Julienne's upset could take away her own joy at having done well in her first competition. The happiness surrounded her in a golden cloud. She floated home in it, and floated to bed, and floated to school in the morning. Six months, six precious months, between now and September to float her way to the training award!

11
Nerves

In the warm September sun, a man stood at the front door of Hooty Cottage with a cat in his arms. The cat's head hung limply, its eyes shut tight, one leg crushed and bleeding. The man knocked again. He was a sheep farmer with thick brown arms that cradled the injured cat.

There was no answer. So he carried the cat back to his Landrover where his friend sat waiting.

"They've gone out with his mother, I reckon. Gone for the day. What shall we do?"

"It *is* their cat, isn't it?"

"Yes. It's little Anda's cat."

The farmer sighed heavily. Bella had streaked across the lane in front of him, and he hadn't been able to avoid her. He scribbled a note on an envelope and stuck it through the letterbox. Then away down the lane he drove, slowly, to avoid shaking the cat who lay in the back of the Landrover.

Half past six and a car full of happy people came bumping up the lane. Bill, driving Gran's car, with Lynne in the front and Anda and Julienne in the back singing and giggling.

The qualifying rounds for the training award had been held at a Sports Center about a hundred miles from Elmsford. Despite a sore throat and headache, Anda had performed well. Perhaps well enough to qualify. Perhaps not. The eighteen finalists and their coaches would be informed by letter.

What worried Anda was her bar routine. Not yet capable of anything difficult, she'd felt her sequence was inadequate. At the last minute she'd refused to wear handguards, which she found awkward, and she'd torn the skin from an old blister on her left hand. It stung and smarted under the dressing, and Christie had been more cross than kind.

"You won't be able to train on bars for weeks if you don't look after your hands!" she'd threatened.

The pain didn't help. But Julienne did. She was kind and sparkly, not at all jealous. On the long trip home she'd giggled and played games, taking Anda's mind off the way she felt. Hot, headachy, and certain that she hadn't qualified.

Julienne was staying the night at Hooty Cottage and they'd planned a happy Sunday, picking blackberries and playing with Bella.

"She's usually on the wall!" said Anda as they turned into the gate. "She always sits there waiting for us."

The two girls hunted for her. Anda stood in the yard calling. A cry came from the cottage.

"Oh no, Bill! Oh no!"

Lynne had found the envelope. It said: "Very sorry. Hit cat with Landrover. Have taken it to vet next to Elmsford Stores."

Anda stood in the doorway, looking at Lynne's stricken face. With his arm tightly round her, Bill showed her the envelope in silence. Coldness rushed down her back and through her fingers.

"I wasn't there," said Anda in a tiny, tiny voice. "I left her here alone and she. . . . "

She couldn't bear to think of the little cat's pain and shock. She twisted out of Bill's arms and made for the stairs. He called her back.

"No. Come on. It's no good panicking. We'll get back in the car and go down to the vet. Now."

He led the way outside. Lynne and Anda were both in tears. Julienne followed them, wide eyed.

"She might be okay. Vets can do marvelous things these days!" Bill was saying.

But Anda's mind burned with thoughts of Bella suffering, her delicate bones broken.

She let Lynne take her into her bedroom and remove her shoes while she lay crying on the bed.

"I can't bear Bella to be hurt. Please don't let it be true, Mum."

First the goats. Now Bella. Bella was dead.

Because of gymnastics.

"She's ill," she heard Lynne say quietly. "You go, Bill, you and Julienne. Go on. I'll stay."

"Poor Bella," wept Anda. "All the time I've been training and Bella was here by herself. This morning she came and meowed and she didn't want me to go. And now she's been killed."

Lynne put a thin hand on Anda's forehead.

"You'd better try to get some sleep," she said. Anda slept deeply and could not be woken. When she did wake up it was two o'clock in the morning.

"Bella!" she thought instantly and got out of bed. Next door she could hear Bill snoring. She sneaked downstairs, surprised to see the glow of a light.

"Julienne?"

Julienne looked up in surprise. She was kneeling on the rug with a large cat basket in front of her.

"Come and look," she said. "You won't believe it, Anda. She's actually purring."

"Purring?"

Anda stood at the bottom of the stairs, too scared to look in the basket.

"It's okay," said Julienne. "You come and look. Come *on*. Don't be scared!"

"I wasn't!" Anda crept to look. "Oh!"

She hardly dared to touch the silky fur.

"Don't pick her up," said Julienne. "She's had an operation. The vet's put a steel pin in her leg. She's just coming round from the anesthetic."

Dumbfounded, Anda saw Bella's front leg. The shaved fur. The row of stitches. There was no blood, and Bella looked clean and fluffy. Anda reached out and gently stroked the top of her head.

"She's lost two teeth, and she was badly stunned," went on Julienne. "But the vet says the rest of her is okay. He X-rayed her. She'll get better, Anda."

Anda gulped. With one finger she stroked Bella's ears.

"But — but her leg! How can she run about?"

"She will. The vet said he'd done lots of cats and dogs before and they can all walk about okay. She might limp for a bit. We've got to keep her warm because she's in shock."

"It's a miracle!" breathed Anda.

In the morning when Bella opened her yellow

eyes and looked at Anda, it seemed even more a miracle. The cat stood up gingerly and stretched. She hopped out of the basket and staggered towards the kitchen.

"Oh, poor Bella!" Horrified to see her so wobbly and lame, Anda rushed to pick her up.

"No, leave her," said Bill. "She's got to learn to walk again. And she's still dopey from the anesthetic."

Anda poured out a saucer of milk, and Bella's fluffy tail went up. She was starving!

"Cats have a remarkable recovery rate," said Bill. "Oh look, she's washing. That's a good sign."

"And you, young lady, are having a quiet day!" Lynne said to Anda. "You've got a temperature! Look at her face, Bill."

"Hi, beet-face!" said Bill.

Overcome by an intense headache, she returned to bed and Julienne played by herself in the Hooty Stream and picked blackberries for Lynne.

"I'll tell Christie you're sick if you don't make it tomorrow," she said when she came up to say good-bye. But Anda hardly cared. All day she got worse and worse. There was no question of her going to school tomorrow, or to Ferndale.

The doctor came, bouncing and grumbling up the lane in his car.

"She's got a nasty virus," he told Lynne. "Keep

her in bed for a few days, and out of school for at least a week. And she must rest. No gymnastics."

Anda had been training too hard, and worrying. Four hours a day, through the summer heat, and three times a week at Ferndale. Now that school had started again, intensive preparation for the training award had exhausted her.

The doctor prescribed some horrific pink and red capsules, and Lynne crept about with hot drinks.

Lynne carried Bella up and down the stairs, and Anda, when she wasn't sleeping, spent hours leaning over her box talking and gently stroking. The cat's bright face and silky fur still seemed miraculous.

"I should be training, Mum," Anda kept worrying.

"You've *got* to rest."

"Tomorrow I'll be able to."

"Yes, tomorrow."

The black days chugged past. Wednesday. Thursday and no Ferndale. Gran bringing ice cream. Corngold sun outside.

Saturday. And the postman, with a long white envelope addressed to Miss Anda Barnes. Lynne kept fingering it, wondering whether to let Anda open it or not.

"Come on. Sit up. You've got an important letter!"

She drew back the curtains.

"Do you think this is *it*, Mum?" Anda took the letter.

"It might be a no," said Lynne. "Don't be disappointed."

Slowly Anda peeled and unfolded the paper. "Dear Miss Barnes, I am pleased to tell you. . . ."

"I don't believe it! Mum, I don't believe it! I've been selected for the final!"

Anda let out a scream and bounded up and down in bed. Her head throbbed and she dropped back against the pillows. She and Lynne flung their arms round each other and laughed.

"Oh, Mum!"

But Lynne sobered down. "It's on October 18th. That's only a month!" she exclaimed. "And look at you! Love, you'll never make it."

"Of course, I will, Mum. Don't be silly."

But she was horribly afraid that Lynne was right. She had missed over a week of vital training. By Monday she could eat properly. She got up and dressed, horrified to find her legs like jelly.

Depressed, she sat wondering how she would ever vault again. All she wanted to do was sit on the cottage doorstep in the sunshine and watch Bella padding round in the garden.

"We don't mind about the award," Bill had said. "You get better and be happy."

But Anda cared desperately about the award. Without it her training was going to spoil her parents' life more and more. They had parted with the goats; Murgatroyd was scrapped; and Bill had sacrificed his dreams. The only thing left was to sell Hooty Cottage and move. She had to try!

In the end it was Bella who finally gave Anda the courage she needed. Bella led her, hobbling, right down to the Hooty Stream. She stood up on her hind legs and dabbed at a passing butterfly.

The turf was dry and warm in the autumn sun. Anda sat down. She stretched her legs and pointed her toes. As if drawing strength from the glittering stream and the sunshine, she began her warmups. The long haul back into training had started!

12
The Final

On the eve of October 18th she had a fight with her parents. She had a terrible feeling she was going to fail and she didn't want them to watch.

"Christie will take me. She'll pick me up in Elmsford."

"But we'd arranged to borrow Gran's car, Anda! You *know* we want to go. We'll take you!"

"I just — would rather be on my own."

"I see!" said Lynne icily. "After all we've done for you and your gymnastics, you don't want us there! That's nice, isn't it!"

"It's not like that, Mummy!"

"Well, what is it, then? We've been to your other competitions! I thought you were glad to have someone there to cheer you on!"

"I am but — well, this is special. I feel different about it. I need to be on my own so that I can really concentrate."

"Well, surely the other children's parents will be there?"

"Yes. Some of them. There's not really an audience — only the judges and promoters, I think."

"But we've arranged to have Gran's car! I just don't understand you, Anda! You shouldn't have arranged that with Christie!"

"I didn't. She offered to if I was stuck."

"Well, she needn't. You can come with us, Anda. Gran would be so hurt. She wants to come. Don't you realize how much *she's* done for you?"

"Yes."

Anda sighed, and Lynne suddenly blew up.

"Honestly! You expect everything laid on for you and then throw it back in our faces!"

"No, Mum, it's. . . . "

"All we've given up for you, and then you tell us we aren't wanted! That really does take the cake!"

Shattered and confused, Anda looked at her silently.

"You don't know the half of it, Anda. What we've been through for you! Do you think we like having to borrow Gran's car?"

"I do, Mum. That's *why* I want the training award. And I'm scared of letting you all down."

Bill came to her rescue.

"You won't let us down! We're proud of what

you can do, and the way you've fought back after that flu! I wish I could get it into your thick skull that we don't care about you winning!"

"But if I don't?"

"We'll find a way."

"What way?" asked Anda suspiciously.

"Well — we can't go on borrowing Gran's car. That's a temporary measure. I'll have to repair Murgatroyd myself, and get her back on the road."

"But if I won, you'd have the money for gas to take me there, Dad. And for my training weekends and clothes and things."

"If you won — it would just be a bonus!" said Bill.

"But would you get another goat if I did?" persisted Anda who had never forgotten the shock of the goats being sold to pay for her clothes.

"Well — yes, I must admit I might do."

"He would," said Lynne.

That decided it. She had to win!

When they reached the Sports Center in the morning, the sheer size of it frightened her. Around the arena were stacks of seats, quickly filling up with spectators. Outside were huge posters and a line of people buying tickets.

Anda panicked. "Oh no! It's like Wembley! I didn't know! I thought it was only going to be a few people! Not all this lot! Oh no!"

"You'll be all right!" said Gran. "You haven't got nerves!"

"I have."

Bill gave her a push.

"Okay, we'll go home then," he teased.

"No, Dad!"

"Go on," he said. "And good luck!"

Suddenly glad they had come, Anda ran to find Christie in the warm-up room. Most of the competition squad were with her, including Lena.

"Whatever are you doing here?" asked Anda in surprise.

"Watching you, you twit!" said Lena.

"They've come to cheer you on!" said Christie. "So no coughing on the beam!"

Anda grinned. She still had a cough and was hoping it wouldn't interfere with her performance.

"You'd better get in your seats," said Christie and the squad moved off, unfamiliar in dresses and jeans. Kerry had even made a Ferndale flag to wave.

Completely overwhelmed, Anda sidled up to Christie. "Christie — I don't know if I can. I didn't know it would be so — so huge!"

Christie looked down at her. "Anda!" she said reproachfully. "You're not going to chicken out, are you?"

"No, of course not."

With a chest full of hammering nerves, she got changed.

Julienne was there suddenly, full of chatter, doing Anda's hair for her. "There's a display after the competition!" she bubbled. "Christie thinks it's something I could do! Modern rhythmic gymnastics."

"You'd be good at it!" said Anda.

A glance into the stadium made her nerves worse. The beam and bars looked somehow ominous.

"What a crowd!"

"It's not *that* many people!" said Julienne. "It's not really like Wembley. You've been used to the little group of parents we usually get!"

"I'm even scared to go in for warm-up!" said Anda. "I wish you'd come in with me."

"I'm not allowed! Look, it says only coaches and competitors. I'll go and sit with your mum."

"All right. Tell her she's not to shut her eyes when I vault!" replied Anda, reluctant to let Julienne go. "And — don't tell them I'm scared."

"Why not?"

" 'Cause Dad thinks — they all think I've got guts. Only I haven't really. Not today!"

Christie came sweeping in.

"Aren't you warming up yet? Come along!"

"See you. Good luck!"

Julienne disappeared round the corner. Anda looked up at Christie. Didn't Christie have any idea how terrified she was? Apparently she did, for she hurried Anda into the arena. Once she'd started warming up, she soon got used to the rumble of talking people. An hour's warm-up. Then march-in and presentation.

"Anda Barnes. Age eleven. Ferndale Gymnastics Club."

Step forward. Stretch. Wave. Try to look happy! Somewhere in that beach of people sit Bill and Lynne, and Gran. The Ferndale flag is waving. You've got to win!

"Penny Green. Age eleven. Park Gymnastics Club."

"Heidi Adam. Age eleven. Sandhaven Gymnastics Club."

Her two rivals! Penny, black-haired, ponytailed, full of bouncy confidence, and Heidi, solemn-faced, bobbed hair, and bamboo legs. Next to them, three eleven-year-old boys. Then the ten- and twelve-year-olds.

The hall pulsated with rhythmic clapping as they marched off to sit beside the performing area.

"You're first on bars, Anda!" Christie met her with a program in her hand. "Come on. Back in."

"Oh no, Christie!"

The asymmetric bars were her worst discipline.

And she was to be first to stand alone in the huge stadium and begin! Christie was fixing her hand-guards, adjusting the bar for her. No backing out now!

"Anda Barnes, on bars," boomed the announcer, and a nerve-splitting hush fell on the audience. Gran's heart thudded across the hall. Lynne shut her eyes.

"Concentration," whispered Christie.

The bars. And only the bars. No hall. No people. No Dad. No Gran. Only bars.

With swift precision, Anda found herself doing her bar routine, her limbs going like clockwork, straddling and catching, circling and swinging. Then her underswing dismount, arched and high from the top bar. A blur of Christie waiting to catch her if she needed it. Her feet bolted to the mat, her aching body forcing itself to stand swallowlike to finish.

"I don't know what I did," she said breathlessly to Christie. "I just sort of — went mechanically. What did I do?"

Christie gave her a hug. "You did okay. It was kind of — fast! But as good as you've ever done."

But when Anda saw Penny Green's performance, her hopes fell. Penny did far more difficult moves than her, and did them expertly. Anda could have wept with sudden, unreasonable disappointment.

Heidi was even better.

Overcome with gloom, Anda sat twiddling her hair, talking quietly to Christie.

"They weren't that good!" Christie said encouragingly. "And don't forget it's your overall score, not just the bars!"

Anda gritted her teeth and smiled at Penny and Heidi as they moved on to the beam.

The terrible nerves had calmed a little. Depression had set in. Her five-point-eight on bars was pathetic compared with the sevens the other two had scored. Again she was to perform first on beam.

A pause while the judges argued on a score. She looked up, and suddenly spotted Gran, Bill, and Lynne. Three tense faces, and Julienne's full-moon smile. Kerry was holding the homemade flag high above her head. She thought how Kerry had fought back after her illness. She thought of Bella climbing the stairs with such courage. And her own courage flooded back.

Don't you let this go, Anda Barnes! she thought.

The judge was ready for her.

"Anda Barnes on beam."

A neat straddle mount. Forward roll. Still there!

Arabesque, turn, cat-leap. Now her forward walkover. She was lucky! With a fifty-fifty chance of falling, this time she completed it and stayed upright. Dance, slide to splits, pose. She even felt steady enough to put extra style into her dancing. The time whistle blew and she quickly did her barani dismount. She heard Christie shout: "Yes!"

Applause. Wolfwhistles from her dad. Julienne's braids whirling.

Now for the marks.

Tensely she and Christie stared at the marks board while Penny warmed up.

"Seven-point-nine-five."

It meant nothing until the other two had finished.

"She hasn't got as much amplitude as you!" whispered Christie as Penny began her beam exercise. It was no more advanced than Anda's, and she wobbled twice and fell once. Then Heidi made a complete mess of hers, falling three times and overrunning her time. Two low scores brought the three girls almost even.

"You've got a chance now, Anda! You really have!" said Christie, with her magical smile. "I never expected you to do this well! You could win, you know! You could!"

"I was lucky on the beam. My walkover!" smiled Anda, the excitement rising inside her.

"There's often an element of luck! But more often it's the way you respond to this kind of situation," said Christie. "Or you could lose by half a mark."

"No."

From that moment Anda believed she could win. Her handspring vault was strong and clean. But Penny, with a beautiful yamashita, finished one whole mark ahead.

"It's you or her. There's no way Heidi can catch up now!"

Now only the floor exercises lay between her and success or failure.

Tiredness was creeping into her. She still had a cough, and the stress of the long afternoon was taking its toll. Her leotard felt prickly and one of her wrists ached. Beads of pain shot up her arm when she put weight on it. To her annoyance Christie insisted on wrapping it for her.

"I can't *dance* with a great bandage thing on!"

"Rubbish. Everyone does. You see Olympic girls with bandaged knees and things."

"But I'll look horrible!"

"You won't."

"I will, Christie, and it's too tight! I can't flex my fingers freely!"

"If it's not tight it won't help."

"But Christie!"

"Don't fuss!"

She had no choice but to wear the hot white wrist support.

"You must *not* let it put you off, Anda! Come on, you're getting tired. Where's that fire in your belly?" coaxed Christie.

"It's — still there!"

"Good girl. Warm up now. Five minutes."

Five precious minutes to limber and stretch, and hate the bandage on her wrist!

And then the little girl from Hooty Combe stood waiting at the corner of the mat. The mass of people looked down, and saw her birdlike face, big brown eyes, and golden ponytail. No longer a child who cried and smashed things and ran away, but a gymnast, cool, disciplined, and full of corked-up fire.

"Open your eyes!" hissed Bill up in the audience. "You are to watch this, Lynne!"

Lynne opened her eyes.

"Anda Barnes on floor."

Her music began. Space-age music, full of power and sparkle.

Holding hands very tightly, Bill and Lynne watched the tiny figure in the purple leotard. Round off, flic-flacs, back somersault.

"Oh heavens!" murmured Gran.

And Julienne sat with her braids twisted round

132

both hands, heart thudding for her friend.

Anger at wearing the wrist bandage helped to give her extra height, extra stretch. She danced and flew like Thumbelina, while her parents clutched each other, not breathing.

Poetically she finished on the last twang of music.

Bill, Lynne, Gran, and Julienne stood up and cheered. Even Gran behaved like a football fan, dropping her glasses and clapping wildly.

Anda walked off with a weird feeling of finality. The cheers died away. She shook. Nothing mattered until Penny's score. Penny was leading by one mark.

"Just don't be disappointed," Christie kept saying, as they waited for the white numbers to appear.

Her own score: seven-point-nine-five.

And Penny was walking out to begin.

In the longest minute of her life, Anda sat looking up at her parents and Gran, thinking of Bella and Hooty Stream. Thinking of everything but Penny's performance. To lose by half a mark!

In a cocoon of gloom she sat. Whatever happened, she must smile, and congratulate Penny, and steel herself for the final march-in.

Tension. Silence.

Then a roar from the crowd, and Christie suddenly swept Anda off the bench and hugged her.

"You've done it! You've done it! You HAVE!"

"What?"

"You've won it! By half a mark, Anda!"

She stood there. "I can't have!"

Christie laughed.

Anda looked across at Penny and saw a pale, defeated face. Only then did she believe it. She'd been too uptight even to look at Penny's score.

"But she's better than me," she said to Christie.

"She wasn't today."

Impulsively Anda rushed up to Penny and took her hand. "I'm sorry," she said. "Was it important for you — the award?"

Penny shrugged. "Well — no, not that desperate. I'll get a medal. Was it for you?"

"Yes. Very desperate."

"I'm glad, then. Well done."

"Yes, well-done!" added Penny's coach warmly.

"We'll meet again — at other competitions!" said Penny. "I'll beat you next time!"

Standing on the podium receiving her medal was a unique moment that would live forever. With her gold token medal was an envelope containing the precious details of the award. She waved it high and the applause pounded in her ears. Bill whistled, Lynne wept, and Gran beamed with pride.

Then they were marching out. The boys in white. The girls in colored leotards. The hall throbbing. The rhythmic display team ready to march in. Julienne rushing towards her. The moment of glory still bright in her heart.

Far away in the chill of autumn, Hooty Cottage twinkled expectantly. The stream sang and the birch trees danced with golden leaves.

On the gatepost a little black and white cat sat watching the lane, waiting for her saucer of cream.

About the Author

SHEILA HAIGH was born and brought up in the farmlands of Somerset in England. For a time she taught handicapped children in the London area, but now she lives in the country, where she teaches in a village school. Her interest in gymnastics stems from when she ran her own gymnastics club for children. Sheila Haigh is the author of eight books for children, but *The Little Gymnast* is her first book to be published in the United States.